MURDER ON THE MULLET EXPRESS

Gwen Mayo
and
Sarah E. Glenn

Published by:
Mystery and Horror, LLC
Tarpon Springs, Florida

Murder on the Mullet Express
First Paperback Edition

Gwen Mayo and Sarah E. Glenn, Authors

Sarah E. Glenn, Editor
Darby Campbell, Associate Editor
Cover by Gwen Mayo
Copyright © 2017 by Gwen Mayo and Sarah E. Glenn
Published by Mystery and Horror, LLC

ISBN: 978-0-9964209-7-6
Library of Congress Control Number: 2016915235

This is a work of fiction. Any resemblance to any actual person living or dead, or to any current location is the coincidental invention of the author's creative mind. Historical events and persons are entirely fictionalized within the bounds of what can be imagined without contradiction to known facts.

Dedication

This book is dedicated to Constance Odessa Chambers (1888—1963) and the other members of the Army Nurse Corps. We are grateful for their service and inspiration.

Acknowledgements:

We would like to thank Patricia Winton, Carol Megge, and Darby Campbell for their input. We would also like to thank the First Florida Chapter of the Historical Novel Society for critiquing our work during its creation.

We would like to thank the Citrus County Historical Society and the Homosassa Historical Society for the valuable research they provided.

A special thank-you is also due to the woman at the St. Petersburg Public Library who found the name of the Citrus County sheriff for us.

MURDER ON THE MULLET EXPRESS

Chapter 1

When traveling with Percival Pettijohn, it was best to bring a sidearm. Cornelia was glad that she'd brought hers.

Here they were, broken down on the Dixie Highway in the no-man's-land between Gainesville and Ocala. All she saw were pines and cabbage palms on either side of the rain-soaked highway. Two vehicles had already splashed past, ignoring their waves and cries for help. If a car stopped, though, would it hold assistance, or thieves who had decided to pluck two old crows and one old coot?

"What is the world coming to?" she muttered. "When I was a girl, no driver would have left a stranded motorist in the middle of nowhere." It was irrelevant that the only motor car she'd seen as a girl was a steam-powered monstrosity built by her Uncle Percival.

The hood of her Dodge Brothers Touring Sedan was up and her uncle bent over the motor. Cornelia hoped that he could do something to get it running again, even if his expertise was in steam engines. There'd been plenty of steam when he lifted the hood. Great billows of metallic-tinged clouds still assaulted her nostrils and moistened her iron-gray hair.

The countryside around them was deserted, probably a good thing. Since they'd passed the Florida state line, they hadn't traveled for more than an hour at a time without passing a chain gang of shackled prisoners at hard labor. She pinned a loose strand back into the bun at the base of her neck, and leaned over the motor beside her uncle.

"Any luck?"

"The water pump is leaking. These automobile manufacturers know plenty about gasoline combustion, but they should have bought the water cooling system I patented in 1923. Would have saved us a great deal of misery."

"Humm," she mumbled. His invention sounded like a screaming banshee, but Cornelia wasn't about to tell him that. "Can you fix it?"

"If I were in my shop and had my tools, it would be no problem." He scowled and added, "I was not permitted to pack everything I wanted to bring."

He glanced at Teddy, who leaned against the side of the sedan. She was reading a ponderous tome with a puzzled expression on her face.

"Did she have to bring two cases?" Uncle Percival asked, wiping his face and smoothing his short white beard. "Plus a sewing kit and a book large enough to claim its own seat?"

"Don't worry; your new motion picture camera was sitting on its lap." The tripod took the rest of the space. Traveling with the two of them, Cornelia counted herself lucky to have one carpet bag for herself. That was jammed between their mountains of luggage in a way that made it impossible to keep her two suits and single evening dress from wrinkling.

"She needs diversions that allow her to sit, Uncle. Her lungs don't tolerate exertion well. The second case holds her medicine."

"One flask of medicinal alcohol?"

"One flask wouldn't last a week, and you know it."

He straightened, no longer frowning.

"Oho. Mr. Scroggins has supplemented her again? No wonder she's embroidering curtains for our local bootlegger."

"A man who has a private stash of bourbon barrels in his cellar shouldn't be criticizing other people's drinking. Besides, I'm sure she could be persuaded to share."

To keep the peace, if for no other reason.

Cornelia glanced down the road again. At least they were close enough to a city for paved roads. That narrow ribbon of pavement was the only modern innovation in an otherwise savage jungle. A thin cloud of fog hovered inches above the wet ground. The desolate stretch of road and the scent of decaying foliage reminded her of her early days as an

2

army nurse in San Juan. She wasn't young any more. Neither was her uncle.

Why was he so stubborn? He could die down here, between the pneumonia he caught from his Thanksgiving trip to Arkansas, the arduous car drive from wintry Kentucky, and the damp air. He was determined to make the trip despite his poor health, and was certain that nothing would befall him with two nurses in his entourage. The man was fooling himself. At his advanced age, a bevy of nurses couldn't keep him going many more years.

Another car approached from the other direction. It was one of the new Cadillacs.

Teddy set the book aside. "Perhaps I should show some leg this time." She posed in front of the breakdown and hiked her skirt an inch.

Her legs were still lovely, Cornelia thought, but the silver curls peeking out from under the red cloche hat might put the wolves off. To her surprise, the Cadillac slowed and parked in front of them.

"Works every time." Teddy was smug. She reached up and poked an errant tress back into place. "I should have tried that earlier."

A young man climbed out of the car, straw hat in hand. He jammed it on his head, obscuring a shock of sandy hair.

"I heard that you were broken down. Has anyone offered to help yet?"

Someone had told him that they were stranded? Cornelia's mouth curled down. "Have you come offering your assistance for money, sir?"

"No, ma'am. I don't own a tow truck. But I thought you could use a ride. It's not very far to Ocala from here." He hesitated. "I'm sorry; I should have told you who I am. Peter Rowley, land agent." He stuck out his hand.

"What a coincidence," Teddy said. "We drove down for the grand opening in New Homosassa."

"I thought that might be the case, when I heard that a car from Kentucky had broken down on the highway," Rowley said. "I'm selling several plots there, so it was in my best interest to come see if you were potential customers, although I would have helped you anyway."

"How sweet of you to offer," Teddy said. "We appreciate it."

Cornelia was unsure of the arrangement, but at least she understood his motives. She did have a gun if he turned out to be an expert liar. Strictly speaking, the M1911 hadn't started out as her sidearm. The army issued sidearms to their doctors, but hadn't seen fit to issue them to nurses. A young officer she saved insisted his was better off in her hands than his own. Cornelia hadn't traveled without it since.

"And you three are—?"

The old man bowed slightly. "Percival Pettijohn at your service, sir. Retired professor from the University of Kentucky. This is my niece, Cornelia Pettijohn, and her companion, Theodora Lawless."

"Glad I could help. You ladies might want to bring your valuables with you, since your car will be alone for a bit. I could even fit a suitcase or two—"

Uncle Percival was already tugging the tripod out of the back seat, and Teddy had yanked her 'medicine' case out the other side.

The Cadillac had an impressive amount of room. Everything from the Dodge fit, even Teddy's steamer trunk, although the trio wound up sharing seat space with the smaller items.

Rowley glanced at the green sedan as he pulled out onto the road. "That is a fine car. I've never seen one with embroidered curtains before."

"I made those," Teddy chirped from the back seat. She sat on her sturdy Rimowa suitcase. "I thought the car needed a woman's touch."

"Charming and talented, too? Marvelous." The suitcases shifted as the car picked up speed, dislodging slender Teddy from her perch and landing her in Cornelia's lap. "So, all three of you are coming to the opening?"

Uncle Percival nodded as he adjusted the amplification of his hearing aid. "I've been considering a winter home for a while, one in a milder climate." He studied the wet yellow grasses whizzing past. "Wildflowers at the end of January. Impressive. Do you get frost here?"

"Rarely," the young man assured him.

"Excellent. I'm getting a little long in the tooth for ice and snow."

The garages in Ocala were closed for the weekend, but Rowley got one to open for the three travelers. It was clear that he considered them his customers now. He even waited with them while the mechanic went after their car.

Cornelia had trouble getting the garage owner to understand that the sedan was hers, especially when Uncle Percival kept interrupting her to tell the poor man his business. It was of no consequence to him that she had managed on her own through three wars and the Pancho Villa Expedition. The lovable old coot had to be in charge. She decided that if they presented her uncle with the bill, she might make him pay it.

Rowley helped them find lodging for the night, which was no easy chore. Most of the hotels were filled with other attendees of the opening. When he announced that he had procured reservations, Cornelia expected to be boarded in some tiny inn on the outskirts of town. He must have done an extraordinary sales job; their rooms were a suite at the Ocala House. Within minutes, they were unloading the Cadillac in front of a stately brick hotel in the center of town.

The real estate agent stared at the mound of luggage the hotel staff wheeled away. "I didn't think that you ladies would be able to fit everything into the car, but you did. You're remarkably efficient packers."

Cornelia smiled for the first time that day. "It's not hard when you have to be. In the Great War, nurses weren't afforded much room or time on the front. Teddy and I are retired army nurses, well, nearly retired in my case. I'm on leave until I muster out in May."

The young man's grin was genuine. "Really? I served in the war myself. Alsace. Where were you stationed?"

"Verdun," Cornelia said. Where Teddy had fallen to mustard gas. Lungs damaged, she had retired from the Army with a disability pension, while Cornelia had continued to serve for nearly another decade. She had begun taking more of her accumulated leave in the last year; first, when her mother passed away, and now, chaperoning her uncle in Florida.

"I hope you weren't one of our patients," Teddy said.

"Not me, ma'am, but some of my buddies were. A bunch didn't make it. One of them was my brother."

They exchanged sober glances. The tragedies of the French battlefields were past, but always present.

Professor Pettijohn broke the silence. "The mechanic told me that they would need to order a new water pump. We won't be able to drive in to New Homosassa tomorrow. Mr. Rowley, could we impose on you, or perhaps one of the other attendees?"

"I'm sorry to say, sir, that my car will be full of equipment and I'll barely have room for my assistant, but getting there from Ocala isn't a problem. There's a train leaving for Homosassa tomorrow afternoon."

"A train? I'd heard that the railroads had embargoed everything but food and essentials."

"That's true, the big railroads have been overwhelmed since the Miami port got blocked, but this is a small local line. It runs passengers and cargo between here and Homosassa. The cargo is mostly fish." Rowley added with a laugh, "It's called The Mullet Express."

Teddy sat on a wooden bench outside the train depot. "Broad boulevards designed to care for every traffic demand traverse the city," she read from the booklet for New Homosassa, "winding parkways lined with palms..."

Cornelia shifted the tripod to her uncle's camera. "We all saw the brochure last night."

"I'm just reviewing the information before we arrive."

Uncle Percival waved to his niece. "Come over here with that, my dear. I want to get a full shot of the train."

That wouldn't take long. Rowley oversold the Mullet Express when he called it a small local line. The train consisted of an ancient engine that belched smoke and cinders, a coal car, a couple of old Pullman passenger cars, a gondola laden with some kind of bins, and a mail car that doubled as the baggage car. The pile of luggage waiting on the platform for loading grew as she watched.

Nearby, Cornelia's uncle fussed with his Eastman motion picture camera, pausing to wipe imaginary dust from the brass-mounted lens. It had been his Christmas gift to himself. The professor was determined to document every detail of their trip on film. At every state line, he had insisted that she and Teddy stand near the sign and wave. Teddy enjoyed being the focus of attention, but Cornelia considered every moment in front of his camera an imposition.

"Ah, steam engines," he said. "So much more dependable than those newfangled diesel ones. I wonder if this locomotive uses that valve array I patented? It was the industry standard for a good twenty years."

Teddy resumed examining the advertising literature Peter Rowley had given them. That was much safer than giving the professor the opportunity to expound on mechanical engineering. "Look," she said, "they already have a theater—how nice."

"Why don't you go back to reading Gertrude Stein?" Cornelia grumbled.

Her companion shuddered.

"I've been reading it since we began the trip. Or, I should say, I've tried to read it. It gives me a headache."

Cornelia's eyes widened. Teddy, bested by a book?

"Maybe you'll be able to read it once we arrive in Homosassa. The roads have been rough in places."

"The problem's not in the reading. It's in the understanding. I've tried my best, but I think I'm just going to throw it away before we get on the train. It takes up so much room."

"After the amount of money you paid to order it? That would be wasteful." Cornelia reached for the book. "Let me have it. I'll read it myself."

Teddy smiled at this. "You didn't like Joyce. Stein's writing style is somewhat similar."

"Joyce was a man. This is a woman. It makes all the difference."

"Just warning you, dear."

"Consider me warned."

Teddy fished in one of her bags and pulled out the fat book. "Prepare for shell shock."

Uncle Percival returned with the tripod, camera still attached.

"Take charge of these, Cornelia. I want to speak to the conductor."

Cornelia set the book aside so she could break the apparatus down, but decided instead to try the machine for herself. She'd watched her uncle use it often enough over the past month. She aimed it at the baggage car, where her uncle was strolling past a woman having an animated discussion with the baggage handler. She was sure her uncle would like having footage of himself with the conductor, so she began turning the crank. Once she was comfortable with the motion, she moved it in a slow pan towards Teddy.

Teddy's response was a smile and curtsy. She hiked her skirt an inch.

Shouts broke out behind her, and she turned, dropping the hem. Cornelia shifted the camera to follow her glance.

Chapter 2

"You bounder!" a man's voice shouted. "I should have known you would be here!"

Through the viewer, Cornelia now saw two men circling each other near the entrance of the first passenger car. One, a burly man with a heavy mustache, held his fists in a boxing stance, while the other had his arms up in a defensive pose.

"Cheat! Thief!" The aggressive one swung, and his opponent jumped back. People began gathering—to watch, of course, not to stop the fight.

The first man lunged and gained purchase on the defender's sleeve. He closed in.

"Let go of me, you—" The second man stabbed at the mustached man's eyes with his free hand.

The burly man responded with an uppercut to the defender's solar plexus, sending the man to his knees.

"That was quite a wallop!" Teddy sounded impressed, rather than dismayed. Cornelia wasn't surprised.

The first man moved in for another punch, but the conductor, who had come running to the site of the fracas, blocked him. The baggage handler hoisted the second man to his feet.

"What's this, then?" the conductor demanded. "There'll be no fighting on railroad grounds. Do I need to summon the railway police?"

"No," the first man said as he picked up his hat and put it back on his head.

The conductor turned to the second man, who was straightening his clothes. "And you, sir? Do you wish to swear out a complaint?"

The second man stared at the first for a moment, and then said, "No."

"Then no more fighting. You," he pointed to the first man, "ride in this car. And you—" he pointed to the second, "ride in that one. If either of you cause another disturbance, you get bounced from the train, even if we're riding through a bayou. Have I made myself clear?"

Both men gave the conductor a curt nod. They glared at each other before they parted ways, and the crowd began to disperse.

Teddy sighed. "I guess it's over."

"Good. Maybe the train will leave soon," Cornelia said, continuing to crank the handle. She did another long pan of the train and the station behind it.

Her companion perked up again. "Hey, did you get all that on film?"

"Of course."

"Your uncle will be so jealous that you got the fight on film and he didn't."

"That's what he gets for playing with trains. He loves them. Did I ever tell you that he used to have one running around inside his house? It was quite the little marvel. His housekeeper would load his dinner into a steam tray in the top of the baggage car. Uncle pulled a cord at the table and the little train would come chugging out of the kitchen to serve dinner."

"Really? He's never mentioned it. The way your uncle likes talking about his inventions, I'd think he would have a grand time telling me that story."

"Don't ask," Cornelia said, "unless you are prepared to spend the day listening to him lecture on efficient fuel consumption and the mechanics of heat distribution."

Teddy chuckled. "I'll keep that in mind."

Their passenger car was crowded and stuffy in the afternoon sun. The conductor tried his best to sit groups together, but it wasn't always possible. The two women found a seat to share, but Uncle Percival sat two rows back, next to a teenage boy visiting Dunnellon with the rest of his large family. Fortunately, the professor had his new camera on his lap, which gave them something to talk about.

Teddy fanned herself with the Homosassa paper. "I hope the heat won't be too much for the professor."

Cornelia smiled. "If he could manage steam engines in Kentucky summers, I think he'll survive a two-hour train ride. Besides, once we're moving there should be a breeze from the windows."

Passengers filed past them, bags and voices both bumping into Cornelia's space.

"Will there be a beach? Then why are we bothering with this place?"

"If no passengers or freight are allowed on or off the train at some stops, why do they make stops at all?"

"He has no business keeping it, and I'm going to get it back if I have to pry it from his cold dead hands."

"They ought to have paid the railway to make this a non-stop run. Does getting mail on Tuesday instead of Monday really make a difference in a backwater like this?"

The tripod that Cornelia, once again, had been left to hold got jarred and jarred again. Would she be carrying it for the entire trip?

She turned to Teddy. "Please set this against the wall next to you before I beat someone over the head with it."

Cornelia leaned back in her seat and opened the Gertrude Stein book. It didn't take long for her to realize Teddy was right; the book was a morass of repetitive phrases. People were listening and loving, regular and pleasant, sometimes gay and sometimes not as gay. Who had decided that this was literature? Cornelia's idea of literature was Jules Verne.

Worse, the book was giving *her* a headache. She had to finish it, though, or Teddy would tease her. Plus, it would be a huge waste of money if no one read it.

A man swayed past them, gripping the seat backs for balance. His face was pale.

"That's one of the men from the fight." Teddy watched the man with professional concern. When he reached the end of the car, he entered the lavatory.

"He looks the worse for wear," Cornelia said.

"He should. The other fellow gave him quite a sock to the stomach."

When the failed pugilist swayed their way on his return trip, Cornelia laid a hand on his arm. "Are you all right, Mr.—?"

The man forced a smile to his sweaty features. "Janzen, ma'am, Raymond Janzen. Still walking, a good sign. I really need more sitting time, though. Thanks for asking."

Cornelia went back to parsing text about hunters who weren't hunters when, once again, the unfortunate man came up the aisle again, faster this time. He disappeared into the lavatory and did not emerge for a while.

His face was ashen now. Not a good sign.

The train stopped in Dunellon, and the Professor lost his young companion. His new seatmate became Mr. Janzen, who had decided to move closer to his now-preferred lavatory location for the remainder of the trip. Cornelia made a mental note to seek him out again when they arrived in Homosassa. Someone should urge him to seek out a physician. There was a chance he was bleeding internally.

They reached their destination in the early evening. The passengers marveled at their surroundings as they stepped onto the platform. They stood within a circle of electric light in almost cavernous surroundings. Stalactites of Spanish moss dangled from the tallest live oaks Cornelia had ever seen. Branches covered the town in a dark umbrella. Beneath the sound of released steam, she heard frogs croaking. A glint of water shone through palm fronds.

Professor Pettijohn pulled his watch from his pocket and checked it against the clock in the station. He nodded with satisfaction. "Right on time. Admirable, considering the number of extra passengers on today's run."

"Not many street lamps for a planned city of 100,000 people," Teddy said. "Shouldn't the train station be on the White Way they're building?"

"The station was here first," Uncle Percival said. "We are in Homosassa, not the new development. We'll see that tomorrow."

Cornelia wasn't interested in railways or street lights. The place was wonderful, mostly because it was the end of the line. She needed a break from traveling.

Her enchantment was broken seconds later by the glare of automobile lights. A line of cars and a few carriages waited outside the station to take them to their respective hotels. Uncle Percival had booked them into the Riverside Lodge for three nights. This was the first stop on his itinerary. The professor planned to be in St. Petersburg by February fifth— his birthday—to see the construction on the new pier. Only an engineer would enjoy viewing construction work as a birthday activity.

Teddy took her arm. "Look, there's the man from the fight. He must be glad to be off the train."

Jerked back to the present time, she searched the crowd for Mr. Janzen. There he was, being helped into a car by Peter Rowley and a young man who followed him into the vehicle. Good, he wasn't traveling alone. Perhaps the West Coast Development Company had a doctor available, if there wasn't one in the old town.

"Riverside Lodge" consisted of a large Victorian house on the waterfront, five long log buildings set back amongst the trees, and a general store on the dock. Uncle Percival had secured rooms for them on the first floor of the main house. Cornelia stowed her bag in the room and went back to help Teddy with hers. Despite Teddy having to freshen her makeup, the two women were ready for dinner long before Uncle Percival appeared in the lobby. He had taken the time to bathe, change suits, and groom his short snowy beard.

The meal was served *al fresco* by the river. The scent of citronella oil and camphor battled with the deep earthy aroma of the river. Although the stone patio extended the full length of the lodge and all the way to the river, the trio was unable to locate a free table.

"Pardon me," a male voice said, "If you would like to sit with us, you're welcome to." The speaker was a slender man who appeared to be in his early forties. Next to him sat a woman of similar age, presumably his wife.

"That's very gracious of you," Teddy replied. They made their way to the table.

"William and Rosemary Carson," the man said. "We hail from Virginia. And you are—?"

"Percival Pettijohn, retired professor. This is my niece, Cornelia Pettijohn, and her friend Teddy Lawless. We drove down from Kentucky. Unfortunately, our car broke down outside of Ocala."

"Mr. Rowley rescued us," Teddy said.

"He must run a full-service operation," Carson said, adding a chuckle.

"What did you teach, Professor?" Rosemary Carson's heavy brown hair was pulled back into a French twist. The torchlight gave it a gold-red cast.

"Mechanical engineering. I began teaching at the University of Kentucky when it was still the Kentucky Agricultural and Mechanical College. Back then I *was* the engineering department."

Cornelia watched him subtly adjust the volume on his hearing device with the amplification control in his breast pocket. It was probably hard to sort out one conversation with so many going on around them.

A waiter arrived at their table with a tray of sweaty glasses and a carafe of water. He set the glasses down carefully. "Welcome to Homosassa. May I bring you some other beverages while you study the menu? Lemonade, iced tea, coffee?"

The professor pointed at the menu. "What's this mullet spread?"

"A local favorite, sir, a Homosassa special," the young man replied. "Cream cheese blended with smoked mullet, a type of fish caught in the river over there. It comes with crackers."

Uncle Percival nodded. "I'd like to try some. It will fortify me enough to read the rest of the menu."

"Make that two orders," Carson said. "We could also use some fortification."

Cornelia and the Professor chose to drink lemonade, while Teddy and the Carsons ordered the iced tea.

The spread was delicious. The professor ordered another helping to share with his companions, plus red snapper for himself. Carson chose the venison, while the ladies united on the duck with marmalade sauce.

Hellos arose from a nearby table. Peter Rowley had joined some of his customers for dinner. Tonight, he looked overheated in his dinner jacket. Cornelia was sympathetic—the only thing harder than traveling with a crowd was herding them.

"Rowley," William Carson called, "The conductor on the train told me that mullet wasn't a fish."

The land agent grinned. "Oh, he did, did he?"

"Well, is it a fish or not? It certainly tastes like fish."

Rowley pulled back the empty chair at their table, sat in it. "It depends on if you're scaling one or paying a fine for fishing out of season."

"Fishing out of season?" Carson looked amused.

"Yes. Some young fellas down in Tampa got caught fishing for mullet out of season. Their attorney argued that they hadn't broken any laws, because mullets weren't really fish."

Even Cornelia was curious now. "On what basis?"

"Because mullets have gizzards. No other fish, at least any the judge knew about, have 'em. Only birds have gizzards, so the lawyer argued that mullet had to be a type of bird."

"The gills and scales didn't make a difference?"

"They got off without having to pay the fine."

Carson laughed. "That was some sharp lawyer!"

Rowley turned to better face the other man. "Are you a sportsman, sir? Hunting, fishing?"

"I've done a little hunting in my time."

Rowley waved his arm in an expansive gesture. "This area is a real paradise for hunters and fishermen. Ducks, quail, doves, turkey, black bear, some deer. All varieties of fish. The tarpon, the black bass, the crevallo—"

"And mullets," Teddy said. "Or do those count as waterfowl?"

"They pull mullet up by the netful here," Rowley replied. "Remember the train you came in on? When it leaves at six thirty tomorrow morning, the flatcar will be loaded with bins full of nothing but ice and mullet. That's why they call it the Mullet Express."

Uncle Percival yawned.

"I'm sorry," the land agent said, taking his cue. "I'd forgotten how late it was. See you—" he addressed the diners "—see all of you bright and early tomorrow. I've got plenty to show off."

"I don't know if buying a house here would be wise," Teddy said as she hung her dresses in the wardrobe. "It's not nearly as built up as the brochure suggested."

"We haven't seen where they're building yet. Besides, not everything needs to be built up," Cornelia replied, unrolling her stockings. "Quiet is its own tonic."

"This is even more isolated than Fisher's Mill. Only one store, no library, no sign of any nightlife—"

A shriek from the shared bathroom interrupted Teddy's litany. The nurses dropped their respective projects and rushed to the door.

When Cornelia opened it, a young woman fell backwards into her arms. The girl screamed, and it was clear that she was the source of the first cry.

Cornelia stood her back on her feet. "What's wrong?"

"It's horrible!" she managed.

"That's hardly helpful," she snapped, and left her for Teddy to manage. Cornelia stepped into the frame of the bathroom door.

The opposite door was also open. An older woman with salt-and-pepper hair stood there, scanning the room with frightened eyes. The chamber behind her was strewn with clothing and hatboxes.

"Careful," she said, "there's a creature in here."

"Creature? Where is it?"

"In the bath. A reptile or a snake." The woman shuddered.

"Let me look." Cornelia slid into the room, eyeing the crevices and corners with suspicion. At any moment, she might need to jump back if it were a poisonous snake.

The first and second corners were empty; a toiletry bag obscured the third. A strong chance of enemy action there. The fourth corner was hidden by the tub. She glanced over the top.

A small lizard blinked up at her. It was probably a gecko. Cornelia leaned on the edge of the sink and reached for the bath towel. She flung it over the creature, bundling the reptile inside.

"Coming through!" she shouted, carrying the wad of fabric into a hallway crowded with curious guests. "Out of the way, or I'll drop this lizard down someone's trousers!"

The crowd parted like the Red Sea, and she charged through the exit and onto the grounds. One snap of the towel, and the unwanted guest skittered into the bushes.

"I wouldn't come back if I were you," she warned the gecko. "They might make you into a change purse."

The night manager, a Mr. Hoyt, was busy trying to calm his guests. "I'm very sorry, ma'am. I'll check the room myself before you go back in."

"I demand another room! Better yet, another hotel!" The woman with salt-and-pepper hair sounded bold, but her hands trembled.

"Ma'am, you can do what you think best, but I don't have any open rooms, and I don't think any other hotels in the area have an empty room, either."

Cornelia sighed and looked at Teddy, who was trying to hide a smile. "If you'd like, I could check the bathroom regularly for varmints."

"That would be very kind of you, Mrs.—?"

"Miss. Cornelia Pettijohn."

"I'm Helen Minyard, and this is my niece, Kathleen Burnell. We're indebted to you."

I caught a lizard, not a rattlesnake, Cornelia thought, but merely replied, "It's a small price to pay for everyone's peace of mind."

Later, after everyone had returned to their rooms, Teddy and Cornelia pushed the two single beds together.

"That was so funny," Teddy said. "All that fuss over a gecko."

"I remember another girl who made a similar fuss in San Juan. She was quite upset about a gecko."

"That wasn't a gecko; that was an anole. He puffed up his sac and made a pass at me, the masher."

"But you screamed just as loud."

"And you came to my rescue. I don't recall dropping into your arms the same way, though."

"No, you already had me just where you wanted me."

They both laughed.

Chapter 3

Breakfast was hearty. Biscuits, eggs, pancakes, sausage, grits, and all the orange juice the visitors could hold, courtesy of the West Coast Development Company.

"They've gone to some expense on our behalf," Teddy said. "I assume they're expecting a good return."

"We'll see," replied Cornelia. "I've learned a lot about swampland since Uncle began researching Florida."

"Where is he?" Rosemary Carson asked. In daylight, the chestnut tones in her hair were more evident. "Doesn't he need breakfast?"

"Apparently not, although he did ask me to save him a sandwich. He woke me before dawn to have me drag the tripod out so he could take some early morning films."

Their first full day in Homosassa turned warm quickly. A crowd sporting broad-brimmed hats and straw boaters surrounded Peter Rowley and the young blond man at his side. They were assembled on the sidewalk by the river. A launch boat idled at the dock, steam engine hissing and sprinkling the boat's striped awning with cinders.

It was good that Uncle Percival was off exploring. They could do without a repeat of the delay at the train station. He was a dear, but she could just picture him taking the engine of the boat apart while the passengers waited.

Once everyone was on board, the boat puffed out onto the water. Their guide and salesman, Peter Rowley, stood near the prow.

"Happy Groundhog Day, everyone!" As usual, Rowley's grin was fixed in place. "No winter here: that old groundhog never sees his shadow in sunny Florida."

Cornelia thought the statement was ridiculous. Bright light cast the darkest shadows. Everyone else, though, nodded and smiled blandly.

Rowley then introduced the slightly-built youth at his side as Jon Forland, West Coast's 'binder boy'.

"What's that?" Teddy whispered.

"Someone who can take down payments on parcels of land," Cornelia replied, and received shushing sounds from the people on the bench behind her.

While Rowley delivered his spiel, Cornelia looked around at the glassine river, the enormous live oaks, and cedars that enclosed them like the walls of the garden Eden. Palmettos filled the spaces between houses. There, across the water... was that an egret? She lifted her field glasses to look.

As if he'd seen what she was doing—and perhaps he had—the agent directed the crowd's gaze across the river.

"The elegant white house you see over there is the private fishing lodge of several distinguished gentlemen from Atlanta. They've been coming here for decades, sportsmen. Now their secret is yours."

Cornelia shifted her focus to the house, a large Victorian with a broad, well-cared for lawn. "What's the smaller structure?"

"That's a cabin for their chauffeurs. Important men need their drivers, even when they take fishing trips."

The man steering the boat leaned out of his seat. "It's the only place in town colored folks can stay," he added.

Cornelia pressed her lips together. *When Uncle hears this, he's not going to buy a square foot here. Jake would never be able to visit*. Her uncle had practically raised Jacob Mayfield, a prodigy who was now his right-hand man.

Peter Rowley tugged at his collar. His sandy complexion reddened.

"Enough about fishing. I'm more interested in hearing about Dazzy Vance," a familiar man with a thick mustache said.

The land agent recovered. "Ah, the pitcher of the Brooklyn Dodgers. Yes, he's been coming here for the fishing. The team's spring training camp isn't far south of Homosassa.

20

West Coast is trying to persuade one of the teams to make this their winter home."

Cornelia followed a heron in flight, then focused on some waxwings. Tomorrow morning, perhaps she could get out on her own and do some serious birdwatching. Her uncle wasn't interested in her advice on real estate decisions, although he would care very much about what she had learned.

Her birdwatching plans were interrupted by Teddy's elbow. "That was the man who won the fight yesterday. The one asking about baseball."

"Perhaps the fellow he punched was a Giants fan. Very bad sport in that case." She wondered about the other man, the loser. How was he doing today?

The tour group enjoyed a nice luncheon, where they were serenaded by a student band from the University of Florida at Gainesville. Afterward, they endured a lecture on the glories of the soon-to-be-built New Homosassa.

Uncle Percival did not return in time for the motoring tour. The prospective landowners piled into an open-air bus, already half-full of people from a different group. The bus took them down roads with names like 'Fishbowl' and slowed at chalk-lined lots so Rowley could point out their advantages and suggest the type of houses that could be built there. Several plots were already marked as 'Sold', an indication that the opening was successful so far. Cornelia sat at a window seat, studying the variety of trees and wildlife, wind blowing strands of hair loose from her bun. Teddy alternated between reading her brochure and looking out both sides of the vehicle.

They halted in front of a building still under construction. It appeared to be a loggia of sorts, with stucco walls and a tile roof. The land around it had been cleared for paving.

"This is the Arcade," Rowley said. "There's going to be a theater here, plus room for a bunch of other businesses. With the way this city's going to grow, it's going to need stores, restaurants, everything. If you or a family member wants to start a business with guaranteed customers, this is a great opportunity to do it."

"Let's say I wanted to be an entrepreneur," said a beefy man in a cream linen suit and a Panama hat. "I heard there was gonna be a big casino here."

Helen Minyard wrinkled her nose in distaste. Some of their other companions looked unsettled by the question, too.

Rowley tugged at his collar. "There's a place set aside in the blueprints, yes."

"So, are there investors? How does a businessman get involved with that?"

"When we get to our next stop, there will be people you can talk to. They're leasing the space."

Teddy tapped Cornelia's arm. "May I borrow your field glasses for a moment?"

Cornelia handed them over, and Teddy peered beyond the Arcade to each side. She checked her brochure, and then peered down the street again.

Finally, she returned the glasses. "The sidewalk ends just past the hotel and the construction site of the arcade. They haven't gotten as far as the flyer claimed. I was expecting the theater and some shops to be finished. What are we going to do here for two more days?"

The next stop, also their final stop, was in the lot of the new Homosassa Hotel, completed only a few weeks ago. The passengers filed out of the bus and went on a quick tour of the hotel, which was packed with agents and prospective customers furiously negotiating. Young men with folders traveled between the knots of people. They wore knickers, which Cornelia considered inappropriate for conducting business.

Rowley led the group to a table crowded round with people. "Here is the grand design for Homosassa Springs, with lot designations and areas blocked out for parks and other public areas. Some of you gentlemen may be interested in the location of the planned golf course. The pro shop and clubhouse by the hotel are open, though not quite completed."

"Where are the people I need to talk to?" Panama Hat asked.

"Just follow me. Anyone else interested in local business? Come along."

Cornelia spotted her uncle. He was using his barrel-chested build to good advantage as he edged up to the table for a good look at the plans. Cornelia needed to warn him about what she'd learned, but this wasn't the place for it. She waited off to the side. Patience was a virtue one developed as a nurse.

Or, perhaps it was only a virtue a nurse *should* develop. Teddy had wormed herself into a good vantage point at the table too, peering through the spectacles she was usually too vain to wear in public. Perhaps she was looking for an amusement that had actually been built.

Cornelia also spotted Mrs. Minyard. The older woman was grasping the arm of the young man Cornelia had seen getting into Janzen's car the night before. He, too, wore the disreputable knickers, so perhaps he was another binder boy. Both appeared upset. Perhaps she wanted a guarantee of a house without reptiles. The young man nodded in agreement to something, and left.

A short time later, the young man in the knickers re-entered the great hall. "*Gibt es ein Arzt hier?*" He wiped his sweaty face and tried again. "Is there a physician?"

Cornelia approached the lad. "I am a nurse. *Eine krankenschwester.*"

"Come. Please."

She followed him out of the crowded room and up the stairs to a room double the size of the one she and Teddy shared. It was well-appointed with fresh flowers and expensive furniture, but the scent of vomit and rancid sweat told a different story. The curtains of the window and four-poster bed were drawn. A bucket sat close to the headboard on one side.

Cornelia indicated the window. "Please open those. I need light." She reached for the draperies surrounding the bed and pulled them aside.

The man from the train lay there, sunken into damp pillows. His face was nearly the color of his fine cotton sheets. Worse, he did not rouse when she shook his shoulder.

"How long has he been this bad?" she asked the boy.

The youth shrugged. "He was sick last night, but not like this. He didn't come down for his meetings this morning, so I postponed them. *Frau* Minyard insisted on speaking directly to *Herr* Janzen today, so I came up to get him. This is how I found him."

She peered into the bucket next to the bed. An unpleasant sour smell emanated from it. "I see blood here. That's a bad sign."

"Bad?"

"You were right to ask for help. What is your name?"

"Dani. Dani Hegstad." The youth twisted a handkerchief between his hands, tugging, straightening, twisting again.

She wondered why Janzen would hire a binder boy that had trouble with English. "Dani, please go to the front desk of the hotel and speak to the staff. Tell them that this man needs a physician. *Er braucht einen Arzt.*"

"Yes. Right away."

"And come back to tell me what they're doing!" She wondered how long it would take for her uncle and Teddy to notice her missing. With so many people downstairs, they might search for hours. They needed to be informed as to where she was, and Cornelia needed to learn more about the 'wallop' Mr. Janzen had taken the day before.

Teddy, still downstairs, studied the plats for the city. She found the plans for the theater and shopping venues attractive, but few of the projects had even broken ground. There wasn't much of a town to see. New Homosassa appeared to be forming only when people bought property. It certainly wasn't the noble metropolis of the brochure, touted as if it had sprung fully built from Zeus' head.

No, the future of the town depended heavily on selling land to people who were ready to build houses and shops. A number of the people she'd ridden in with on the bus had rushed to buy lots, and were now selling their new purchases shoulder-to-shoulder with the land agents.

Cornelia's uncle pointed to an area of the map and asked about sinkholes, which set the man from West Coast scurrying through his notes. Teddy decided to leave the professor to his fun and find someone to talk to.

The Carsons and Peter Rowley conversed. Rosemary would make pleasant company, although not the exciting kind. Considering Mrs. Minyard's attitude about casinos, she'd be no fun at a party.

Teddy *needed* a party. Her supply of medicinal alcohol was rapidly shrinking, and the extra fortifications she'd purchased from Mr. Scroggins would only last a few weeks. So far, New Homosassa showed no signs of even having a pharmacy, much less a speakeasy. Only parties where they served illegal liquor would keep her going here. She'd spotted a few people who might host those sorts of parties, but they were the same ones who'd left to discuss the casino. Perhaps she could acquaint herself with them later.

Despite the open windows and the spaciousness of the room, it had become desperately hot from the crowd. The binder boys were clever to wear those short acreage trousers; with all the running they did, it was a wonder none of them had fainted.

Teddy stepped outside and found that she wasn't the only one suffering from the heat. Ladies holding fans occupied all three benches, beating the moist air futilely. Men lounged against the wall smoking. She crossed the lawn, looking for an unclaimed sitting spot with some shade. Maybe she would find Cornelia somewhere; the woman had disappeared on her, which was unusual. Cornelia was the reliable sort. Teddy was normally the one to wander off.

As she turned a corner, she noticed smoke creeping around one of the tall hibiscus bushes. A fire? She walked round to investigate, and found Kathleen Burnell smoking a cigarette. The young blonde hid it behind her back and fanned the air.

"Mrs.—uh—I don't remember your name, sorry. Is there something I can do for you?"

"Oh, just curious about the smoke, dear. I was afraid that something was alight that shouldn't be. Don't worry, I won't tell."

"Thanks." She brought the smoldering tobacco back out. "Do you want one?"

The older woman smiled. "No, I've tried them and they make me cough something fierce. I have lung problems."

"Sorry."

"Why aren't you inside with your aunt?"

"Because it's hot. And a crashing bore."

"I agree. I was hoping they would have some of the entertainment venues open for customers, but most of New Homosassa exists only in the minds of the planners. Dreams and future plans are not strong selling points. I could use a real theater about now."

The girl smiled. "Or a beach."

"Yes, a beach. Why haven't they shown us the beach? Perhaps it needs to be built, too."

They both laughed, although Teddy's ended in a cough.

Raymond Janzen, recently of Miami, was one of the many land speculators who had come north to try their fortunes on the Gulf coast. The hotel manager knew very little beyond that. He stood near the door, holding his handkerchief over his nose.

Cornelia suspected that Helen Minyard might know more about Mr. Janzen. She needed to ask Mrs. Minyard what had been important enough to drag the man from his sickbed.

The local doctor was out on a call, so the manager, a Mr. Davis, was forced to drag one of his guests away from real estate negotiations, which amused no one, particularly not the doctor. His name was Duffy, and he had traveled all the way from Maine. The sight of Janzen, though, sobered him.

"This man should be in a hospital, not a hotel."

"I'll arrange it right away, Doctor," Davis said. "The nearest hospital is five hours away. But I'm sure the Company would provide Mr. Janzen a car for the trip."

Duffy and Cornelia shook their heads at the same time. "The trip would kill him," the physician said.

The manager clasped his hands. His knuckles turned pale. "So, what do we do?"

"That depends on what's happened to him," the physician said. "When did he become ill?"

"On the train," Cornelia said. "He was involved in a fight that he lost. He took a heavy blow to the stomach."

"Did you witness this fight?"

"Yes. I even caught it on film," she added. "I can give you a good idea of where he took the worst hit. He spent a good amount of time in the lavatory afterward—that, I can attest to."

Duffy nodded. "An internal injury would explain the blood. If it *is* a bleed, he's lucky that it seems to be a slow one."

"Pupils slightly dilated." He palpated Janzen's abdomen. "Rigidity in the upper region. No guarding—but he appears to be comatose. The only way to confirm an injury here, of course, is surgery. It will have to be done."

"Oh, my God." The hotel functionary was now trembling.

Duffy turned to him. "Your local man may have access to the necessary instruments. If he has a surgery, we could do the operation there."

"Teddy—Theodora Lawless—and I assisted with surgery during the Great War. We are both quite adept at working under difficult circumstances. I offer you our help as needed."

"Thank you, Mrs.—?"

"Pettijohn. Miss Pettijohn."

"Ah, I believe I saw your father downstairs. Rather hard to miss a man who looks like Santa Claus. Please bring your friend here, Miss Pettijohn, so she can offer additional assistance. These are hardly ideal conditions. Mr. Davis, I direly need contact with your town physician."

Mr. Davis found Teddy in one of the staterooms, chatting to some young men about a party. She was unhappy to be interrupted, but came promptly when the situation was explained. The Carsons volunteered to take responsibility for getting the professor back to the Riverside Lodge. Her uncle took exception to being treated like a child, but Mrs. Carson was quick to soothe his affronted ego by soliciting his opinion on the agricultural properties of the area.

When Teddy entered Janzen's room, she set her purse on the window sill and approached the bed. "Oh, my, he is rather bad off."

"To put it mildly," Dr. Duffy said. "Could you show me where the blows landed, Miss Lawless? Your companion has already told me what she saw, but you may have seen it from another angle."

"One landed here," she pointed, "and the big punch landed here. He was trying to gouge the other fellow's eyes out at the time, so the move might be considered self-defense."

Cornelia started to tell Teddy to save her embroidery skills for Mr. Scroggins' tablecloth, but was interrupted by Davis' return.

"I telephoned the doc's wife again. Still out on the river making house calls."

"Then it's just us, ladies," Duffy said. "Mr. Davis, we need to begin as soon as possible."

Preparing the room for the surgery took longer than the operation itself. A clean area needed to be created, and extra lamps were brought in to provide more light as the afternoon waned. Kitchen items were selected in lieu of instruments Dr. Duffy did not have in his bag. This included aprons.

The doctor applied iodine liberally over Jansen's abdomen before making the first brutal cut. Then, he explored for injuries. The women saw blood, but no torn tissue. There was no reaction from the patient.

"Stomach has an ulceration," he murmured. "Perhaps the blow exacerbated a problem that was already there."

The sour odor Cornelia had noticed before emanated from the surgical area now. It was strangely familiar, and she glanced over to Teddy. Her companion's nostrils were flaring, and her brow wrinkled. She was clearly having the same problem placing the odor.

Once the surgery was complete, they covered Janzen and did what they could to make him comfortable, not that he seemed to notice one way or the other.

The physician sat, finally, and let out a great sigh. "Given the circumstances, I think our work was good, but it may not be enough. I expected a tear, not an ulceration. It appears to be fresh, not chronic, and the odor was... unusual."

"Unpleasant," Teddy replied. "Almost chemical."

"I set aside samples for the authorities," Dr. Duffy said. "Chances are that the man he fought with is not Mr. Janzen's only enemy, unless the hothead is also a poisoner."

The physician rose, removed his apron, and went to the private lavatory to wash his hands. When he returned, he picked up his bag.

"Could you ladies stay with him through the crisis? I'll check back after dinner and give you a break. There is really nothing more to be done except to watch and hope he pulls through."

Near the entrance of the hotel, Tiny Belluchi and his pal Cesare smoked, watching the swells arrive for the evening's entertainment. It beat him why anyone would want to buy plots of jungle in a backwater like this, but rich people were goofy. They probably thought it was exotic. The most exotic item Tiny had seen so far was a huge bug he'd suddenly found on his jacket sleeve. Cesare laughed when it took more than one whack to get it off his arm.

There weren't enough skirts here to be interesting. Yeah, there were a few shebas buzzing around, but most of them had come with their sugar daddies. He spotted a girl a bit younger, good-looking, but she was with a real fire extinguisher, probably her mother. Nuts.

He didn't have time for a girl anyway; business always came first with Tiny.

The music had started up in the ballroom. Once it got good and loud, he nudged Cesare and they pitched their butts to the curb. Time to go to work.

A few bucks in the right hands had gotten them Benny's room number. While Benny jawed with the land agents that afternoon, they'd located it. It had nice big windows, and was on the first floor. Well, well. Very convenient.

They circled the grounds until they were standing outside Benny's window. The grass was damp, like everything here after dark, and Tiny's socks got wet while he forced the window open. He detested wet socks; he thought he'd left that problem behind in Chicago.

Once inside, they drew their guns and checked the rooms.

"No sign of him," Tiny said.

"The night's still young." Cesare dragged a padded chair out of immediate sight of the door and plopped into it. "Take a load off your feet. Let's enjoy his room for him."

Tiny wandered to the table instead and began examining the tag on a gift basket. "With regards from the West Coast Development Company."

"Hey, you can read. I wouldn'ta thunk it," Cesare said.

"Don't get fresh. Oranges, honey... Hmm, some cigars."

"Now you're talking. Shall we light up?"

"Not now. He'll smell it from the hallway."

"Give me a few for later, then."

Later didn't come for a long, long time, during which they ate all the oranges. The music from the ballroom ceased well after midnight, and Tiny thumped the dozing Cesare.

"Hey. Party's over. Almost showtime."

They cleared the orange peels off the table and positioned themselves: Tiny at the entrance to the bedroom, Cesare with his back against the wall next to the door.

Fifteen minutes later, they heard the key in the lock. After a moment of fumbling, Benny came in. He was plump and middle-aged. He started to take off his jacket. A dark stain, perhaps coffee, marred his white shirt.

Then he spotted Tiny, who was hard to miss at six foot three. "What the—"

Cesare seized Benny from behind, and Tiny moved in to deal a solid blow to their target's midsection. The older man would have bent double if not for Cesare's grip. They pulled him to the floor, and Tiny clubbed his head with the gun until he stopped moving.

"Time to take out the garbage," he said, rolling Benny over. "Grab his feet."

They hoisted the body and stuffed it out the window. Time to get their feet wet again.

The convulsions began in the wee hours of the morning. Teddy's shout roused Cornelia from her light sleep, and she lurched out of the wingback chair near the fireplace. They held the wracked body onto the bed by sheer body weight while Cornelia bellowed for help.

The spasms continued for several minutes. By the time the night manager entered the room, Janzen was dead. A fine foam trickled from his mouth.

"Fetch Dr. Duffy," Cornelia ordered.

The manager turned and fought his way through the crowd that had formed outside the door. The entire floor seemed to have assembled for Janzen's final gasps.

"You must call the police," Dr. Duffy told a red-eyed Davis, who still wore his pajama top under his jacket.

Davis just stared. Cornelia pitied the man. He was probably prepared for his well-heeled guests to pull some antics, but this wasn't something the maids could mop up after.

Dr. Duffy tried again. "You do have police here, don't you?"

"I—I'm sorry, sir. I was hoping that this was just a bad dream."

"Don't we all? Sadly, it is quite real. This man is dead, and he died either as the result of the fight at the train station or poisoning. The authorities will have to determine which, but either way this is a homicide."

A collective gasp echoed in the hallway, and Davis found his wits. He ran to the door and slammed it shut. "Poisoned? Here?"

"I don't know where he was poisoned, but I believe he consumed something corrosive before his death. Blunt force alone does not explain some of his injuries."

"Oh, God. Pardon me, ladies."

"I think He will understand," Teddy said. "It's been a trying night."

Chapter 4

Morning was well underway when the nurses arrived back at their own hotel. Uncle Percival was having breakfast on the patio. He tipped his hat to them, then studied their faces.

"I assume things went badly."

"Yes," Teddy said. "Our patient passed away."

"The man who was in the fight?"

Cornelia scowled. "Does everyone already know about it?"

"Not much else to talk about here if you're not selling something," the professor said. "And if you are, death is bad for business."

"Indeed," Cornelia said, and sat. Teddy followed suit and pulled a free chair over to hold her purse.

Uncle Percival gestured to the waitress. "Susie! Breakfast for my nieces."

Susie was young enough to still have freckles. Her blonde waves looked like a home job; too much bleach on the ends.

The women ordered their food.

"Do you want that with coffee, ladies?" the young woman asked.

"No thank you," Teddy replied. "I need to get some sleep."

"I'll take some," Cornelia said. "I don't think I'll be able to sleep for a while."

"Thinking about what to tell the law?"

All conversation around them stopped.

Cornelia tipped her head close to Teddy's curly-haired one. "I'm leaving the details to Dr. Duffy. He's the one they're going to want to speak to, and his opinions will carry more weight than ours."

"But we saw the fight. He didn't."

"Teddy, plenty of people saw the fight," Cornelia said. "Although they may want to view the film when it's developed."

"They'll probably come here, but will be more interested in speaking to Mr. Hofstetter first," Uncle Percival said. "I've been watching the hotel office. Half expected to see him checking out in a hurry."

"Hofstetter?" Teddy asked. "Was that the other fellow's name?"

"Yes."

Cornelia decided to change the subject. "What are you planning to do today, Uncle Percival?"

"I've hired myself a boat for the day. I'm going to examine the local terrain."

Cornelia said, "I hope you've also hired a porter for your tripod."

"The owner of the boat will be handling that," Pettijohn said. "Would you like to come?"

She shook her head. She wasn't up to her uncle's level of energy today. "No, there's a river tour today for bird watchers. I meant to go on it, and I think I shall."

"What about you, Teddy?"

Teddy thought about it, then shook her head. "No, I think I'd better sleep. I heard about a party happening tonight, and I think I'd like to try crashing it."

"Be careful where you crash," Pettijohn said. "Not all the predators are in the jungle."

Cornelia settled onto one of the benches near the dock and waited for her launch to arrive. She should have known better than to be early for any event in the South. Between years of army nursing and her uncle's obsession with punctuality, she was well trained in the art of hurrying up to wait. The time wasn't a total loss. She spotted a rare whooping crane feeding in the shallow water at the edge of the river, and a fine pair of wood ducks that the other bird watchers would miss. Footsteps on the boardwalk spooked the ducks. Cornelia lowered her field glasses and turned to see which of her fellow travelers was interested in ornithology.

"I'm sorry. I've frightened your beautiful wood ducks away," Rosemary Carson said. "I tried to tread quietly."

"They'll come back. Would you like to join me?"

Mrs. Carson took a seat on the bench beside Cornelia and removed the covers from the lenses of her field glasses while Cornelia trained a camera on the tall grass across from their lodge.

"I spotted a whooping crane in the grass over there," Cornelia said, pointing to the other side of the river. "He's hiding at the moment, but I'm sure he's still there."

"How exciting. I've never seen one."

Both women were still sitting motionless, focused on the opposite bank of the river, when the bus from Homosassa Springs carrying the rest of their bird watching expedition turned into the parking lot of Riverside Lodge. Its screeching brakes spooked the timid crane, causing him to take flight. Cornelia managed to snap a photo just as he rose from the shore. They watched in silent awe as one of the rarest and most magnificent birds in North America disappeared into the distance.

"Meg would have loved that," Rosemary said.

"Meg?"

"My younger sister, Margaret. She and I used to spend hours roaming the woods with our binoculars."

Their launch was rounding the bend. Passengers from the tour bus drifted toward the dock.

"It's a pity she couldn't come with you," Cornelia said, as she got to her feet. "At the rate the whooping crane population is dwindling, there isn't likely to be another opportunity."

A tinge of bitterness crept into Rosemary's voice. "Meg and I won't share any more expeditions." Her gray eyes focused on the patch of tall grass where the crane had been. "She died before my eldest was born. When she—my baby— arrived in June, we named her for Margaret. Perhaps she too will develop an interest in birds one day."

"Was it during the war?" Cornelia asked. "The reports all talk about troop losses, but there were plenty of nurses and aid workers that died unnoticed."

"Nothing so heroic," Rosemary said, as they boarded. "The Spanish flu."

"My father died of the same ailment," Cornelia said. "Of course, it was more tragic that so many young lives were lost."

The two of them found seats together on the launch and settled in to listen to their guide, a tall man with thick white hair that stood in stark contrast to his sun-bronzed skin and dark eyes. Cornelia could tell that several of the ladies found him handsome by the way they crowded each other to sit near him when there was an abundance of better seats further back in the launch. She wondered if they were serious bird watchers, or just there to take a pleasant cruise along the river.

The Homosassa River tour offered plenty to see, but Cornelia had to settle for watching osprey through her field glasses. Their preference for nesting high in dead trees kept them too far away for a decent photograph. She did manage to get pictures of several types of gulls, a trio of brown pelicans, and a magnificent shot of an anhinga perched on a boulder with both wings spread wide to dry in the morning sun. By the time they returned to the hotel, she and Rosemary were chatting like old friends. It had been a long time since she had exchanged sighting stories with a companion who shared her interest in ornithology. Teddy thought birds were pretty, but lacked the patience to wait for the shy ones to venture near.

Teddy washed the makeup off her face before lying down. She napped for a little while, but was awakened by a tapping on the door.

"Miss Pettijohn? Miss Lawless? Are you there?"

It sounded like Helen Minyard. Teddy put on her dressing gown and headed for the door. "Just a moment—I'm coming."

Mrs. Minyard had surrendered her dark clothing in favor of a lilac print. She held a straw hat in one hand. "I didn't mean to wake you. I'm terribly sorry."

"That's perfectly all right. What's going on?"

"Kathleen and I are going on a boat excursion to the Gulf. We thought we would invite you and Miss Pettijohn to accompany us."

Teddy was surprised, as Mrs. Minyard didn't strike her as very sociable. Perhaps it was Kathleen's suggestion. "How lovely! Thank you for thinking of us! I'm afraid Cornelia isn't here, but I'd love to come. Give me a moment to change."

"Certainly."

Teddy popped back into the room and grabbed a sundress, her Mary Janes, and a suitable hat to protect her face from the sun. After dressing, she applied Hinds cream to her face and a little lip rouge, but left it at that. Too bad Cornelia wasn't here to see how quickly she could get ready in the proper circumstances. She tucked the container of cream in her bag before joining them in the lobby.

"Are you sure there won't be swimming?" Kathleen was asking her aunt.

"I'm sure if swimming were involved, they would be advertising it. Ah, Miss Lawless, you're just in time. People are gathering at the dock."

There were several motorboats available, which was convenient. Each came equipped with its own land agent, which was very convenient for the company. Teddy chose the one with Peter Rowley, since she thought he wouldn't spend their time pushing a hard-sell.

The three women boarded and chose seats. Kathleen sat to one side of Teddy, Mrs. Minyard on the other. Once the benches were full of passengers, they took off, following the other boats down the river and into the mangroves. Teddy pulled the drawstring tight on her hat's mosquito netting.

Mrs. Minyard's parasol jounced when they hit the wake of the other vessels. Kathleen held onto her hat. Teddy gripped the rail so she wouldn't slide into the girl. Soon, they were negotiating breaks between clumps of mangroves. Birds darted from branch to branch.

Rowley began directing the attention of the men to the water. "That's snapper. Sheepshead are also plentiful this time of year. The trout should be running in Crystal River, too."

He was met with appreciative murmurs.

"And over there," he said, pointing, "is a manatee. You may know it better as a sea cow. Do you see its shape, deeper in the water? They move into the springs here during the winter because the water is warmer. The Seminoles used to eat them, but the Florida Legislature made it illegal to hunt them about twenty years ago. I've heard, though, that the meat is like beef or pork."

As Rowley continued his presentation, Mrs. Minyard turned to face Teddy. "I'm sorry we disturbed your rest, Miss Lawless."

"Teddy."

"Teddy, then. I heard that you and your... sister? were called to render aid last night."

"Yes, the poor man."

"What happened to him?"

"Aunt Helen," Kathleen whispered from Teddy's other side, "don't be morbid."

"Was he the one that was in that awful fight?"

Ah, it was a matter of gossip. It was the first vice she'd seen in the woman. What a relief. "Yes, it was him. I'm afraid he passed away."

One of the men across from them seemed discomfited, so Teddy changed the subject. "Peter," she asked in a louder voice, "is there a place to swim here?"

"Oh, there are a number of swimming holes in the area. There are several large springs. Crystal River has some very good places."

Kathleen followed Teddy with her own question. "Is there a beach?"

For once, Rowley hesitated before answering. "Not with sand, no. There are some beaches a short drive south of here. We have beautiful waters, though, and this area is a natural wonder. Freshwater fish and saltwater fish intermingle here, and the water is so clear in the springs that you can see them."

"Are the alligators saltwater or freshwater?" Teddy asked, pointing one out. The men were immediately interested, but Mrs. Minyard and one of the other women screamed.

"Don't worry, ladies, we're safe here on the boat," Rowley said. "Wood doesn't taste good, and there's enough fish for everyone. To answer the question, Miss Lawless, they prefer fresh or brackish water. Once we're in the Gulf, we'll be out of their territory and you'll have a splendid view to enjoy."

He was correct. When they emerged from the mangrove islets, a vista of blue-green water spread before them. The sky was a brilliant blue with tall white clouds. Murmurs of appreciation blended with the hum of the motor.

The tour boats followed one another into the Gulf, a strand of pearls on a bolt of turquoise moire. Teddy wished she had the professor's camera, or even Cornelia's Brownie, to capture the calm waters and the view of the shore. Of course, neither were capable of capturing the color. Only an artist could render the shifting hues of green, blue, and aqua with any justice. For the first time, she felt that Homosassa had its attractions.

"How did your river safari go?" Teddy asked the professor at dinner. The three sat with the Carsons again. "Did you get some good shots?"

"Some excellent ones," he said. "There are a number of islets on the river, little chunks of land entirely surrounded by water. Some of them have houses on them, and their residents' only route to town is by boat."

"No bridges?" Cornelia asked. She was still tired, even after a short nap that afternoon.

"Oh, a few, but not many. Around here most people travel by boat. There's a little town north of here, Ozello, where the public school is on one of the islands, and the children are ferried to class every morning."

"How exotic," Teddy said. "Is Ozello any more built up than Homosassa?"

The professor smiled. "The terms the developer would use are unspoiled and pristine."

"I could go for unspoiled," Cornelia said. "This area is a little too pristine for my lights, though. Four or five hours to the nearest hospital?" She pictured Uncle Percival falling ill, or Teddy developing a cold that worsened her lung affliction. The lack of facilities here would be as deadly for them as they were for Mr. Janzen the night before. When dinner was over, she really needed to have that private conversation with her uncle.

The professor had continued his narrative, oblivious to his niece's reverie. "And the fishermen were preparing the mullet for shipping. Chopping the heads off, gutting them, and tossing the bits into the river."

"Ugh! What a horrible thing to do to the water," Rosemary Carson said. "I shan't be taking any dips in the river."

"You wouldn't want to swim here anyway. The show was well attended by an aquatic audience—gulls, pelicans, and alligators."

"I saw a few alligators on our trip to the Gulf, but that was at a distance," Teddy said. "How large were the ones you saw?"

"Most were around ten feet long, but a few were easily eleven or twelve feet."

"Weren't you worried about being in the same river on a relatively small boat?" Rosemary asked.

"That's why my guide had the shotgun and rifle," Uncle Percival said. "He didn't seem very worried. He told me that alligator was rather tasty."

"Oh, the flavor isn't bad," Cornelia said, "but the texture is a bit on the rubbery side. Given a choice, I would take a nice shark steak over alligator any day."

The professor's bushy brows rose and he gave his niece an appreciative glance.

"Really Cornelia, you surprise me sometimes. I had never thought of you as an adventurous eater."

"She wasn't all that adventurous with the snails in France," Teddy teased.

Cornelia's posture became more rigid than usual.

"I tried the snails when they were served. No matter how much garlic and butter our French hosts put on them, they still tasted like peat moss."

"They were a delicacy," Teddy protested.

"You can call dirt a delicacy, but it's still dirt."

The professor laughed. "I had never considered how many exotic delicacies you had the opportunity to sample in your travels. You must find home cooking somewhat pedestrian."

"Not at all. I'd trade a month's pay for Momma's fried chicken, mashed potatoes, and an unhealthy portion of her blackberry cobbler with homemade ice cream."

"That sounds like a meal that would be worth a month's pay," Mr. Carson said. "I haven't had blackberry cobbler in ages."

"You haven't *picked* blackberries in ages, dear," Rosemary said. "If I recall correctly, you were complaining about chiggers and snakes the whole time they were in season."

After dinner, Cornelia took her uncle aside. She told him what the tour boat driver had said about the chauffeurs' cabin being the only place a man like Jake Mayfield would be allowed to stay.

Professor Pettijohn's face flushed and, for once, he didn't look like Santa Claus. "This new Klan is worse than the old one. In my day, they didn't try to mix it up with Christian morals. Now people think they're doing God's work when they tread on their fellow man."

"I'm so sorry," she said. "But I knew you would want to know. Do you think we should leave tomorrow?"

The old man thought for a moment, then shook his head. "We only have one more day here, and it's paid for," he said. "Besides, our car is still awaiting repairs. I called the garage in Ocala this afternoon, and they're still waiting for the part. They think it may arrive tomorrow."

"They *think*?" How long would it be? And when had it become 'our' car, rather than *her* car?

"They're blaming the rail embargo, of course. We may need to inform the Vinoy Hotel that our arrival in Saint Petersburg has been postponed."

Chapter 5

Mr. Rowley and a uniformed man close to the same age but a bit thicker around the midsection stood there when Cornelia opened the door. She wasn't sure how well Rowley knew the officer, but there was no trace of his usual good humor. He looked downright uncomfortable.

"I'm sorry to bother you ladies at this hour, but Andy— Deputy Andy Davidson needs to speak with you both. He's been taking statements from witnesses to the fight on the train, and, I guess, to Mr. Janzen's final illness."

Cornelia glanced back at the beds, neatly separated again. No unmentionables in sight. "Ah, of course. Please come in."

Davidson turned to his companion. "I need to talk to the witnesses alone. I'm sure you understand, Pete."

A glance of barely controlled hostility passed between the two, then Rowley left.

"You two know each other?"

"Went to school together," the deputy said, and pulled out his notebook. "Now, you are Mrs.—"

Grr. "Miss. Miss Cornelia Pettijohn."

"Right. You were the first one who went upstairs when the victim took sick."

"He'd been sick for a while," she corrected. "Since the trip on the train."

"I see," the deputy said, writing a note. "Did his illness begin before or after the fight?"

"I didn't take notice of him before the fight began," Cornelia said. "Once we were enroute to Homosassa, it was clear that he wasn't feeling well."

"When you say 'it was clear', what do you mean?"

"He was pale, diaphoretic—"

Deputy Davidson looked up from the notepad. "Dia-what?"

"Sweating a lot. Even for a packed passenger car in Florida."

"Ah." He wrote another note.

"He visited the lavatory with increasing frequency, and remained longer each time," she added.

"Did you know him personally?"

"No."

He raised an eyebrow. "You seem to have paid a good deal of attention to him."

"I am a nurse. I have earned my living by paying attention to such things for more years than you have been alive. It is second nature to me to notice signs of illness."

"Besides," Teddy said, emerging from the bathroom in a shimmering dress of peacock colors, "I was watching him, too. He'd been in a big fight. We thought he might have been seriously injured."

She turned her back to Cornelia. "Zip me up?"

Deputy Davidson had the grace to blush at the sight of the exposed skin and ladies' foundation garments.

"You're rather flashy tonight," Cornelia observed. "I'm surprised you're not wearing the red dress, though."

"I'm saving that one for the Professor's birthday on Saturday. We need to do something special for him." She plopped on her side of the twin beds and began stuffing her feet into tiny pumps, giving Davidson a flash of garter that Cornelia hoped was accidental.

The deputy's eyes were definitely averted. "Yes, your uncle. I'll be interviewing him next. Do you know why the fight started?"

Cornelia blinked. "No. Why?"

He made a note. "Witness doesn't know why the fight started."

Teddy, fully dressed, came over. "Neither do I. So, why were they fighting?"

"That's neither here nor there."

"Nonsense! Motive is very important," Teddy said, adjusting the beaded bandeau adorning her silver hair. "You should speak to Mr. Hofstetter. He was the one who punched him, and I'm sure he had a reason."

Davidson closed his eyes and gripped the bridge of his nose. Cornelia turned to hide a smile.

"Please, Miss—"

"Lawless."

"I've already interviewed Malcolm Hofstetter. I want to know what *you* saw and heard. Sheriff wants a complete report."

"Oh. Well, I heard him—Mr. Hofstetter, as I found out later—call Mr. Janzen a bounder. He also said something that sounded like his presence at the station wasn't a big surprise. I don't remember the precise words."

Davidson made yet another note. "Did Janzen say anything?"

"Something like 'Let me go'."

"And then?"

"Hofstetter socked him. On the jaw. Janzen fell down, but he got back up on his own. He grappled Hofstetter and tried to poke him in the eyes. Hofstetter shoved him away and gave him a heck of a wallop in the abdomen. Dr. Duffy thought the blow might have caused internal bleeding, but later he wasn't as sure." Teddy stood and smoothed her dress. "He said Mr. Janzen might have ingested something corrosive after he examined the stomach and intestines."

"Mm-hmm." Davidson swallowed uncomfortably and made a note. "Like..?"

"He didn't say. He took samples of blood and stomach contents." She widened her eyes for innocence. "Did he give you those?"

Disgust flashed across the deputy's face. "Yes. The hotel packed it in ice for me."

"I hope you can find out what's in it. The odor from the abdominal cavity was familiar, but I couldn't quite place it."

The deputy's tanned face paled. "I'll leave that to the appropriate authorities, ma'am. Thank you very much for your time."

He beat a hasty retreat. The pair waited until he had closed his car door before they laughed.

"If that young man wants to continue in law enforcement, he is going to need a stronger constitution," Cornelia said. "What's he going to do when the gruesome parts aren't packed for him?"

The ladies joined Uncle Percival outside the lodge, where they awaited their ride to the evening's entertainment.

"Did the sheriff's deputy speak to you yet, Professor?"

"Yes, he did, Theodora. I regret I was unable to be much help describing the fight, since I was examining the train's engine. Mr. Janzen was already ill when he sat next to me, and he didn't stay in his seat very long. By his fifth trip to the facilities he was unable to utter more than a groan, so I gave up any attempt to engage him in conversation."

"That must have been hard on you, Uncle," said Cornelia. "I imagine he made a miserable travel companion. He made a great number of trips to the lavatory. I still wonder about the cause."

She was nudged by Teddy. "It's our turn for a car, finally."

They approached the waiting Cadillac. A man with evening stubble got out of the car. He opened the door for Teddy and Cornelia, then went around to open the far door for the Professor.

"I've seen this type of car before," Cornelia said. "Everywhere, it seems."

"I think it's standard issue from the company," the chauffeur said, climbing in.

"I hope we get there before they start the film." Teddy tapped his seat with her cane. She'd wanted to leave it behind, but Cornelia had reminded her of how many times they'd already had to stand in line for Company events. "How fast can you drive?"

"Plenty fast, ma'am." He revved the car, and they lurched away from the hotel in a spray of crushed limestone. The vehicle bounced on the rutted road, and they reached for handholds.

"If we don't get there on time," Cornelia said, "it's because you took forever with your makeup. Who do you expect to see you in the dark?"

"It's for the party afterward. I hope someone spikes the punch."

"You always hope someone spikes the punch."

The driver muffled a snort with his hand. "Homosassa Hotel directly ahead, ladies. Busy place tonight." Cadillacs lined the curb in front of the grand manse. He pulled their vehicle into the queue.

Teddy clutched her cane. "Perhaps we should get out and walk from here."

"You're awfully eager to see this film," Cornelia said.

"I didn't get to see *The Freshman* when it came out."

"With Harold Lloyd?" their driver said. "You'll like it. It's a riot."

"That settles it. Stop the car." Teddy disembarked and set a swift pace for the hotel, Cornelia close behind. The professor followed at a more sedate pace.

"You're going to wind yourself," she warned Teddy.

"As long as I recover before the party. They're supposed to have a dance band tonight."

Their driver was correct about the movie. The misadventures of Harold Lloyd on the football team had the three of them laughing.

"Splendid movie," Pettijohn said as they exited the hotel's makeshift theater. "I think I had a student or two like 'Speedy Lamb'."

"There were a few like him in the ranks as well. Will you be going to the ballroom with us for the party?"

"No, Teddy dear, I believe I'll return to the hotel for some light reading before I turn in. It's been a busy day, and I trust tomorrow will be the same."

"Oh, for an evening of light reading," Cornelia said after they'd seen him off. "It sounds so much nicer than loud music and dancing."

"We don't have any light reading," Teddy replied. "Just Gertrude."

"Good point."

The band was playing 'Nobody's Sweetheart' when they entered the ballroom. Vases of fresh flowers in vibrant shades of orange and yellow stood on pedestals along the walls.

Knots of people stood on the dance floor talking. All of them were younger than Teddy and Cornelia. A few of them glanced over at the pair, puzzled.

"They probably think that we're here as chaperones," Cornelia said.

Teddy laughed. "We'll just let them know that we're not Mrs. Grundys." She made a beeline for the closest group, Cornelia trailing behind as usual.

"What a beautiful headdress," Teddy said to one of the young women. "Did you have it custom made for you? I've never seen anything quite like it."

Neither had Cornelia. The pink feathers reminded her of the flamingos she'd seen in Cuba during the Spanish-American war.

The girl smiled. "I had it made just for this trip."

"It becomes you," Teddy said.

The two plunged into a conversation about clothing, and Cornelia did her best not to sigh.

One of the young men, a tan fellow with slicked-back black hair, decided to be polite to her. "Are you enjoying the area, ma'am?"

"I'm enjoying the terrain," she replied. "The exotic plants, and especially the variety of birds."

"Oh," he said. "My *abuela* likes birds, too."

"Many old ladies do."

His response was a genuine smile, revealing teeth whiter than his linen suit. "So, how'd you end up here?"

Cornelia returned the smile. "In Florida, or in this ballroom?"

"Both."

"My uncle is looking for a winter home."

He hesitated. "Your... uncle?"

"I know, you're thinking that he must be as old as Moses. If he isn't, he's getting close."

The young man laughed. "I think I know which one. Looks like the American Santa Claus, but with a shorter beard?"

"That's him!"

Teddy turned to them. "And who is this dashing gentleman?" She fingered her long strand of beads.

"I apologize. I didn't ask your name. I am Cornelia, and this is Teddy."

He bowed quickly. "Pleased to meet you both. My proper name is Santiago, but I go by Chago."

"Charmed to make your acquaintance, Chago."

The band struck up 'Let's All Go to Mary's House', and people began to dance. The talkers moved to the edges of the room. Cornelia moved with them, but Teddy tapped Chago's arm.

"Dance with me, won't you? I love dancing, but I can only do it for a little while."

"Of course I will."

She gave her cane and silver clutch to Cornelia. "Hold this for me, won't you? I've got a strong arm to lean on."

Teddy and her dancing. Cornelia couldn't help but smile. Her lungs might fail her, but Teddy's feet never did when she heard a lively tune. She had to be at least thirty years older than any of the other women twirling on the floor, but that didn't embarrass her. It was one of the many things she loved about Teddy.

She scanned the people hovering around the edges of the room. A few of them might be classified as mature, but most were in their twenties. Cornelia spotted a familiar face: Kathleen's. The girl must have slipped away from her aunt for the evening. She'd applied lipstick—albeit inexpertly—and wore a smart sleeveless dress that was long enough for modesty.

The first song ended, and 'The Charleston' was next. A whoop went out, and the floor filled quickly. Teddy kicked next to Chago, delight on her face. Their young neighbor rushed to join in.

A middle-aged man approached Cornelia. "Pardon me, madam," he said, "but I noticed you were sitting this dance out. May I sit it out with you?"

Cornelia studied the man, who had thinning dark hair with white temples. "Certainly. I'm Cornelia. And your name is—?"

"Leo. Are you staying here at the hotel?"

"No, we're in the Riverside Lodge. This place was booked for the entire week."

"It looks it. Are you enjoying your visit so far? Will you be buying into the project?"

Drat. A real adult to talk to, and he was one of the land speculators. "My uncle is the one who will decide about that. Peter Rowley is our agent." That should drive him off.

"Is he here?" Leo's dark eyes scanned the room. "A thoughtless man, to leave you by yourself in a strange place."

"Of course he's not here. He went back to the hotel after the movie. I assure you, I can take care of myself."

She watched him size her up. She'd pinned her hair in a twisted bun this evening; no flapper bob for her. Her gown was the matronly type, black silk with a modest neckline and black lace sleeves. The long waist was a concession to modern style, but even that was belted, though there were a few rhinestones on the buckle.

"I'm certain you can," Leo said after a moment. "Perhaps he brought you because he was in a strange place, then."

This made her laugh.

"He brought us because I own a car," she told him, "and he was too independent to take the chauffeured ride from Jacksonville that West Coast offered."

If there was one thing Pettijohns hated, it was being beholden to others. Family didn't count, though.

"Ah, yes, the rail embargo."

"Our car broke down near Ocala. Mr. Rowley came to our rescue and acquired seats for us on the Express. Not that the Mullet Express is in any way rapid transit. It stopped every few miles."

"Still, it was very good of him. I think I know which one your uncle is. The bearded man with the camera?"

"That's Uncle Percival. The camera was his gift to himself for Christmas."

His eyebrows, which were thick and curly, rose. "Percival?"

She chuckled. "We also have a Gareth and a Roland."

"What about Lancelot?"

"No, but we did have a Galahad. My grandmother had a fondness for knights. And Shakespeare."

Leo grinned. "My mother must have wanted a genius, or at least a good painter for the—" He looked past her. "*Bella signora*, I just saw a gentleman I desperately need to talk to. Would you excuse me?"

"Of course," she replied, but he was already gone. Who was she to stand in the way of a quick sale? He had been courteous enough to call her pretty, though, something she had rarely heard even when she was young.

She turned her gaze to the dance floor and spotted Chago. He was coming her way with Teddy, who now hung onto his arm for real. Kathleen trailed behind them, looking scared.

Cornelia went over and helped Chago lower her to a chair. "Teddy, you should know when to stop by now."

"But I love the Charleston," Teddy said, then gasped for air. "I just didn't know—that so many other songs—had Charleston in the title, too."

Chago's linen suit crinkled as he knelt by her. "It is my fault. I was too vigorous."

"No, I loved it." Teddy began coughing hard, and grabbed the clutch from Cornelia's hand. She yanked out a handkerchief and covered her mouth. The coughing continued.

The burly youth patted her back clumsily. "Should I find a doctor, *Señora* Cornelia?"

"No," Cornelia said, "She's done this before. She loves dancing, but her lungs are not what they used to be." She checked Teddy's nailbeds for her circulation. Waste of time— the nails were bright red with that damned Cutex stuff.

Naturally, Teddy also had lipstick and powder on her face, making her job harder. Fingertips weren't blue, though.

"Do you think punch would help?" Chago asked.

"Yes, get some. It should help with the cough."

The young man headed for the nearest party table, shoving people out of the way.

"Must you do this to me?" Cornelia hissed as soon as he was out of earshot. "You're going to drop dead if you don't learn your limits."

"I don't notice limits when I'm dancing," Teddy said, then coughed again. "It's when—the music stops—that I feel them."

Kathleen asked timorously, "Will she be all right?"

Cornelia started. She'd forgotten about the girl. "Probably—despite her best efforts otherwise."

Their male companion returned with two cups. Teddy took a swig, then another. "Wonderful!" She finished the first cup, and held out her hand. "Next."

"Let me guess," Cornelia said. "They've juiced it."

"Mmm-hmm." She sipped at the second cup. "A vast improvement. Is there more where this came from?"

"Let me make up to you for my exuberance," Chago said. "Some friends of mine are having a private party upstairs later tonight. If you like this punch, I know you'd love a Mary Pickford."

"Mary Pickford? I thought she was an actress." Teddy's cough was already subsiding.

"In Havana, she is also a drink. With cherry."

"Oh," Teddy said, "She sounds very refreshing."

Cornelia unlocked the door. "Stop singing. People are trying to sleep."

Teddy did, then giggled like a schoolgirl. "I think Mary Pickford is my favorite movie star."

"Until you find a drink you like better." She hustled her tipsy companion into their hotel room.

"You make me sound fickle."

"Yes, you're going to break the heart of all those other cocktails you've discarded like yesterday's mail."

Teddy tossed her headdress in the direction of the wardrobe and collapsed onto the bed. After a moment, she lifted a leg so she could pull off her shoe. "I will suffer later for my infidelities."

"Yes. I estimate that will begin in about four or five hours. I'm headed for the bath," Cornelia said. "I reek of cigar smoke."

She ran the lizard out of the tub and wiped the porcelain down. The reptile eyed her while she turned the faucets and adjusted them to the best temperature. The cigar stench permeated her good clothing. Her foundation garments she could wash by hand, but the dress needed professional attention. She put it aside and turned off the faucets.

Her resident gecko peeked at her from behind one of the tub's claw feet. The thought of Mrs. Minyard finding him there made her smile.

Cornelia addressed the little lizard. "And what are you looking at? You'd better leave before the ladies next door wake up. Go on now. Shoo!"

Teddy was still in her party frock when Cornelia returned in her cotton robe and pajamas. At least she'd gotten the other shoe off before flopping backwards on the bed.

"It's stuffy in here," drunk Teddy complained.

"You're just flushed from too much fun with Mary. You'll cool down soon enough."

"No, it's from your bath. All that hot water."

Cornelia went around her bed and pushed it toward Teddy's. "I used tepid water. I wasn't cold."

"I bet you cooked yourself like a lobster."

"No, you're just stewed."

"Don't sleep too close to me. Open the window. I need air," Teddy said. "I'll get sick if I don't have some fresh air."

"You'll get sick anyway," Cornelia said, but reached for the window. She lifted the sill, but it slid down as soon as she let go.

"That wasn't enough air for a mouse. Open it again."

"The darn thing won't stay up."

"Use the book."

Cornelia shrugged and took the Gertrude Stein book off the nightstand. She normally treated books with more respect, but Gertrude lacked respect for her readers. Tugging the window open again, she shoved the book under the sill. "Glad to know it's useful for something."

The voices woke her up. Were the walls that thin? No, they were from outside. She could hear the footsteps. Revelers coming from the same party they'd attended, no doubt.

She still had the window propped open. That was why the voices seemed so loud. Cornelia sat up, and immediately shivered. What was the temperature in here, fifty degrees? In the faint light, she could see that Teddy had crawled under the covers at some point. Time for her to find some extra blankets, and time to close that window.

Her robe and slippers were a minor improvement. She peered outside. Two shadows, one an enormous hulk, tromped across the grass. They were backlit by the distant streetlight. She reached for the book, prepared to close the window on a pair of drunks. Her hand paused when she heard the next few words.

"The old geezer's on the side facing the river. Second from the end."

There was only one true "geezer" in this hotel, and they'd just described his room. These men were looking for Uncle Percival.

There were no telephones in the rooms. She rushed for the nightstand, stumbling over one of Teddy's shoes enroute. Her sidearm and a torch were in the drawer, right beside the Gideon Bible. She smiled, remembering that her father kept a drawer at his bedside with much the same supplies, except his always had a bottle. Bullets, bourbon, Bible, and a torch to light his way onto the road to either salvation or perdition, was what her mother always claimed. Cornelia tucked the memory away and withdrew the pistol.

The hallway was empty when she opened the door, but she didn't trust it to stay that way. Would the invaders enter her uncle's room from the inside entrance, or try to force the window from the outside? They could probably break the window without waking him—the old coot was half-deaf.

She scooted down the hall and tried his door. Locked. Prudent, but inconvenient to her. Cornelia thumped on the door, then began pounding. Peter Rowley poked his head over the upstairs railing.

"What's up? Is something wrong with the professor?"

"I heard men outside. They were talking about breaking into Uncle Percival's room."

Rowley came down, stopping on the stairs when he saw her gun. "What men? What did they want?"

"I didn't ask their names." She continued to pound, and finally the door opened.

The little old man squinted at her, then adjusted his spectacles. "What's wrong? Is there a fire?"

Cornelia pushed past him into the room and turned on the lights. Everything looked as it should—notebook on the nightstand, suitcases stashed away, camera and tripod parked in one corner, and clothing laid on the chair for the morning. Plus, three wind-up clocks. The window was closed and, when she checked, locked. She opened it and peered outside, shining her torch onto the grounds beyond. Nothing. She turned to face an angry Santa Claus.

"Do you mind telling me what's going on?"

She looked past her uncle to the faces in the hall. "Everything appears to be in order. I'm very sorry for waking everyone, but I thought I heard someone trying to get in."

Everyone quickly returned to their own rooms to check for signs of burglary. Everyone except Peter.

His eyes looked concerned. "Are you sure everything is all right?"

"For the time being, Mr. Rowley. Thank you for being so quick to respond. I need to speak to my uncle privately now."

She closed the door and locked it again. It was blessedly warm in his room.

Percival climbed back into bed, pulled the covers over his legs, and put on his hearing aid. "Speak."

"I heard some men's voices outside," Cornelia told him. "They seemed to be taking an unhealthy interest in you. They described an old—older gentleman and where his room was located in this hotel. It was your room."

"Really? How interesting."

"Interesting isn't the word I'd use," she said.

"Did they say they were going to rob me?"

"No."

"Kill me?"

"No."

"Offer to sell me a tropical paradise somewhere else?"

"No! But Uncle Percival, people do not creep up on hotels at—" she checked one of the clocks on the dresser—"at four-thirty-five in the morning with good deeds in mind."

"Your hearing is better than mine. The only thing I've been able to hear from outside are the boat motors in the morning."

Even the earthworms could hear those motors. Cornelia rubbed one frozen foot. "My window was open."

"On a night as cold as this?"

"Teddy was overheated."

He chuckled. "Too much antifreeze again?"

"You know her well."

Chapter 6

Dawn arrived two hours later. Cornelia spent that time napping in the lone chair the hotel had provided for a bachelor's room. Years of sitting watch served her well, but it was still uncomfortable. If they didn't find out what was going on, Teddy might need to trade beds with her uncle so Cornelia could keep an eye on him. No, that wouldn't work. The intruders would come looking for the professor, and find Teddy instead. Who knew what would happen then?

Either they were going to have to find a room for three, an unlikely proposition in Homosassa, or Cornelia needed to learn who was taking such a keen interest in her uncle.

When Cornelia crept back into her own room, her companion was still asleep.

She poked the younger woman's backside. "Wake up, Theodora. We have a problem."

"Uh huh."

"I'm serious, Teddy. Someone tried to break into Uncle Percival's room last night. You need to get up so we can decide what to do." She grabbed the edge of her bed and pulled it away from Teddy's.

The screech of metal on wood made Teddy pull the covers over her head. "Please stop! I'm dying."

"No. You're hung over. Get up. We have a real emergency."

"No, we don't. If he were dead, you would have said so."

"They may have meant to kill him."

"You said 'tried to break into'. That means they didn't," she mumbled from under the covers. "Please go away. Mary Pickford is a real mean Jane in the morning."

"That's what you get for taking advantage of her. I need your help, dear."

The lump under the covers shifted. A mop of tousled silver curls appeared, followed closely by one bloodshot eye. "Could you shoot me in the head first? I'd feel better."

The three of them sat at a small table for breakfast. Cornelia was grateful that none of the other hotel guests had joined them. They needed to figure out who was interested in her uncle and why.

Professor Pettijohn began to order sausage with his eggs.

"That's not a good idea." She indicated Teddy, who was greener than the palm fronds. He wisely switched to bacon.

Cornelia ordered orange juice, eggs, and grits.

Teddy ordered coffee and a bag of ice.

After the waitress left, Cornelia lowered her voice. "Why would someone want to break into your room?"

Pettijohn shrugged. "I brought cash for a down payment. Maybe they wanted it."

"A number of other people here have cash, too. Probably some brought more than you did, especially the ones in that fancy new hotel. Why you?"

"Maybe they have a list, and it was my turn."

"I don't think that's it. If I were that sort of crook, I would break into a binder boy's room, not yours," Cornelia said.

"They wanted to start small?"

She gave him a disgusted look. "Will you please take this seriously?"

The waitress arrived with the coffee and orange juice. She also had a bag of ice on her tray. She handed it to Teddy, who lifted her broad-brimmed hat long enough to tuck it inside.

"There's my camera," the professor said. "It's valuable."

"Most of the visitors can afford one of their own. If they can afford a winter home in Florida, they can afford a camera. Even one as nice as yours."

"Perhaps it's a pair of locals. Men in need of money, and ones who don't have a car. It's a fair walk to the new hotel."

"So, now you're suggesting they picked you because they were lazy?"

Teddy's voice, acidic, broke in. "Figure out who they were first. If you know the who, the why might solve itself."

"Good suggestion," the professor said.

"I need out of the sunlight," she replied. "I thought I'd hurry the two of you along."

"How will we identify these people? What did you see, Corny?"

Cornelia winced at the use of the nickname. "Very little. One was average size, the other was huge. That's about all I could tell."

"But you heard their voices."

"Yes."

"So, we match the voices to the people," he said. "I think we should do some socializing with my potential neighbors today."

"Speak more quietly," Teddy muttered. "I have a fat head."

The professor ignored her. "Should we begin with the people on our floor?" he asked his niece.

"No," Cornelia said, "I don't think they're staying or working at this hotel. We've eaten here every day. I know every voice by now. These men were strangers."

They began their search at the Homosassa Hotel. The largest number of people, and the most talking, was done in the new hotel's lobby or on the covered patio. The three of them had mingled there during their previous visits, walking under the Spanish-style arches or sitting around one of the small tables. They were not disappointed by today's crowd. Groups of people sat at tables, on benches, talking, negotiating, smoking. More than once Cornelia spotted a silver flask being passed discreetly under a table as waiters pretended not to notice. Teddy, fortified with a hefty dose of BC Headache Powder, perked up at the sight of so many people.

What followed was the most boring circuit of conversation Cornelia had ever heard, and she'd been in enough hospital staff meetings to be a good judge of dullness.

A red-faced man with a Midwestern accent was pelting Rowley's binder boy with questions. "So, if I put down fifteen hundred, what return could you get me by next week? There's a property in Clearwater I'm looking at."

Mr. Hofstetter was earnestly talking to a stone-faced couple who appeared dubious of his sales pitch. "The bottom's falling out of the Miami market. No passenger rail, plus that sunken ship blocking the harbor? You'd lose everything buying there. The Gulf is where things are going to boom next. Get in on the ground floor, while the land is still cheap."

"Already trying to resell his own purchase," Pettijohn said, shaking his head as a pair of doormen in smart red jackets held the lobby doors open for him. "Doesn't anyone buy land to live on any more? Yesterday, I saw the same piece of property change hands four times."

Their tour of the first floor was a big zero. Conversation inside the hotel was much the same as that outside. There were sitting areas on the upper floor, Cornelia knew. She decided to leave the professor with Teddy, who was chatting up her new friends from Tampa about the party last night. It was a good thing they'd loaded up on headache remedies before leaving Kentucky. Between Teddy's parties and her uncle's shenanigans, they would probably use every packet before they got home.

She went to one end of the second floor and worked her way down. The first sitting room was all female and working on gossip as much as embroidery. Maybe she would assign Teddy to that detail if it proved necessary. Two men were sleeping in the next area. She couldn't very well poke them awake to hear their voices.

Whispers echoed up the stairwell. "Old coot's down there now with the tippler. They're talkin' to the Cuban. The battle-axe isn't there. On the prowl somewhere, so watch out."

She rushed to the railing and looked down, but all she saw was a mass of moving heads. One of the heads poked above the others, though. It had dark hair and a distinctive bald spot. If she rushed downstairs—

A door clicked closed behind her. She turned, in time to see Helen Minyard leaving Raymond Janzen's hotel room.

Cornelia muttered another curse. Priorities, priorities... *Helen* hadn't tried to break into her uncle's room. That bald spot downstairs, though, belonged to a potential burglar or even uncle-killer. She would talk to Helen later, she told herself as she rushed downstairs, oxford heels thudding on each step.

She descended into the great room again and scanned for the head. Standing on tiptoe, she saw what could be her prey moving towards the double doors leading outside. Luckily, most of the men here were sitting.

Teddy was still talking to Chago, apparently known as "the Cuban". That fit with his reference to Havana at the party. She zigzagged between the tables, fumbling for the gun in her purse.

The daylight temporarily blinded her when she emerged from the doors. She moved back into the shadow of the archway and scanned the area through the slits of her eyelids. There was the large man—at least she thought it was the same one. If she could only see the top of his head to be sure...

To be positive, though, Cornelia needed to hear the voices. The big man and his buddy were speaking to a third fellow. The third man wore a double-breasted suit and, based on his perspiration, was not accustomed to the climate yet. He wiped his forehead, and she saw the curly eyebrows. It was Leo, the man she had met last night.

The bulk of a lingering taxi helped her move in closer without being seen. The young woman entering the cab had a parasol, and Cornelia envied her the fashion accessory. It would have made excellent cover.

"The old bats are buzzing around him like he was Nosferatu," one of the men said. It could have been one of the voices, but—

"How far do ya want me to take this?"

That was him. Definitely the large man. The other speaker was probably his companion from the attempted burglary, although she was not as positive about that.

"As far as it takes, after we get what we want."

It was time to fetch her uncle and find out if he knew the men.

"We've been invited to another party tonight," Teddy said when Cornelia rejoined the conversation. "And Chago says they can arrange a special celebration for the Professor's birthday, if he's not in such a hurry to get to St. Petersburg."

"That's very nice."

"I told him that I don't keep the same late hours Teddy does. Early to rise, and all that." The professor sounded diffident, but Cornelia suspected that he was secretly pleased.

"How old will you be, *Señor* Professor?"

"Seventy-five."

"Again," Cornelia said. "He's been celebrating his seventy-fifth birthday for a while. I think he likes the number."

"Did you return just to make fun of your elders, Corny, or did you find something out?"

"At the rate you are aging I'll soon be your elder, Uncle *Percy*, but if you have a free moment, I did find them."

The professor frowned. "Please excuse us, Mr. Aldama."

Once they were out of earshot of their erstwhile friend, Pettijohn asked, "Don't call me 'Percy'. Did you find them?"

"Yes, I did. I only hope they're still outside."

The trio went to the exit doors, and Cornelia cracked one open. To her horror, the doorman pulled it fully open, nearly landing her face first on the patio. She recovered in time and tried to look as though she hadn't been creeping about.

"We're in luck. They're still there," she said, pointing toward the three men clustered together under a live oak. "The one I heard is easy to spot. He's huge."

Teddy and the professor glanced around one of the archways for a peek. Uncle Percival withdrew first. "I presume you mean the gorilla and his two swarthy companions?"

"Yes. Do you know who they are?"

"No. What about you, Teddy?"

"I saw one of them at the party last night. Well, he wasn't actually at the party, more lingering around the doors. He tried to crash, but Chago ran him off."

"The older one's name is Leo," Cornelia said. "An Italian."

"It was the young short one," Teddy said. "That big one would have been hard to miss."

A voice from behind interrupted. "May I be of assistance?"

They turned. A young man in the uniform of the hotel staff stood there. He looked curious.

"No," Cornelia said curtly.

"Yes," Teddy said. "Leo told me he was going to introduce my niece to his nephew, there. The fellow who makes Jack Dempsey look small. Do you know his name, perhaps?"

Their new companion peeked out. "No, although I've seen him around. Why don't you just ask him?"

Teddy checked the name on his jacket. "Well, Edward, I was hoping to learn something about the young man before Kathleen meets him. My brother is a bit on the overprotective side." She twirled her beads. "If I were to give you a little tip, do you think you could find out his name?"

Edward glanced both ways, then nodded. "You can't be too sure, ma'am."

They found some free chairs to sit in as they waited.

"You have a real talent at prevarication, Theodora."

"Thank you, Professor."

"I'm not sure he meant it as a compliment," Cornelia said.

Perhaps Leo's chance conversation with Cornelia hadn't been a chance conversation after all. He'd learned where they were staying, and her uncle's name. A dollar or two in the right hand at their hotel could have procured directions to the room.

They sought out the Homosassa Hotel's restaurant to have a late lunch. Over tall sweating glasses of iced tea, they discussed what they had learned.

The hulk outside was one Martino Belluchi. He had arrived by car on Sunday evening, and shared his room with a Cesare Ricci. Leo, also known as Leonardo Mazzi, had an adjoining room and was paying for their stay. All three hailed from Tampa, Florida.

"Do any of the names ring a bell?" Cornelia asked her uncle. "Have you ever visited Tampa?"

"No to both of those questions," the professor said.

Teddy stirred her tea idly. "Do you think we should tell the authorities about these men? Perhaps that deputy that came by yesterday?"

"I don't think he's going to be interested in hearing from you again," Cornelia said. "You had too much fun with him yesterday."

"I couldn't resist. He seemed so officious, and he plainly didn't like Peter."

"The feeling was mutual, I suspect."

"Speak of the devil." Pettijohn craned his head to get a good view out the window. "The deputy's out on the sidewalk with our man, and neither of them look happy."

Teddy leaned over and nudged the window further open.

Voices, becoming increasingly heated, floated through.

"Confirmed it with Jennings Bowden," the deputy said. "He was at Alsace too, you know."

"Yeah, I know."

"That swindler was the same Quartermaster Janzen you wrote Alice about. The one that sold the ammo out from under your unit. Don't pretend to be stupid."

"It's been a long time. I've been busy with a lot of people. This is the biggest event the county's had in years, Andy."

"You were on the train with him. Yeah, that other guy had a beef with him over the Aladdin City bust in Miami, but this is your blood we're talking about."

"I was in front of dozens of witnesses, plying my trade. I didn't even ride in the same car, for God's sake. What do you think I did to him?"

"What that doc thinks was done. Poisoned him. Whaddaya say?"

Rowley took out a pack of Old Golds, lit one. "I wouldn't have poisoned him, I'd rather have shot the bastard. Strangled, punched him, maybe. But I didn't do any of those things, because I was trying to make a living."

"Says you. I think the sheriff will disagree. If I were you, I'd get a better alibi than 'everyone saw me in the other passenger car'. Everyone saw Janzen, too, and look where it got 'im."

Another sheriff's department car pulled into the hotel lot. A slender man of middle age climbed out of the driver's side. He strolled up to the two men.

"Sheriff Bowden," Davidson said. "I was just questioning Mr. Rowley. Has some new evidence come to light?"

"No, another body."

Chapter 7

Teddy was gone from the dining room before Cornelia could advise her to stay put. The sheriff was headed for the hotel office. The deputy and Rowley followed a couple of steps behind.

By the time Uncle Percival and Cornelia arrived at the office, a crowd had gathered. Cornelia plunged into the crowd.

She found her companion near the front, watching the sheriff read the hotel register. Mr. Davis stood behind the desk, wringing his hands.

"What's up?" she whispered to Teddy.

"The new dead person was a guest at this hotel—just like Mr. Janzen was. Do you think we've had another poisoning?"

"If "we" have, we're leaving town today. If Uncle Percival can't book our hotel rooms earlier in St. Petersburg, we'll find another place. We'll sleep in the car if we have to."

"You're being overly dramatic."

"*I'm* being overly dramatic?" Cornelia hissed, drawing stares.

The sheriff copied some information from the register and slid his notebook back into his pocket. He faced the crowd.

"I hate to be the bearer of bad tidings, folks, but one of the guests here has been the victim of a crime."

"What was the crime?" William Carson asked. His face was pale.

"A Benedicto Cardona was found dead in a boxcar of the Mullet Train. Somebody killed him and stuffed his body into a fish bin. A deputy called me from Ocala; he was looking for bootleg whiskey and got a nasty surprise. The only place that bin could have been loaded on the train was at the station here. We don't know which one of the fish houses filled this particular bin, but we will soon enough."

A buzz ensued, and he waved it down. "I have no reason to believe that the crime actually happened at this hotel, but I could surely use your assistance in tracking the movements of Mr. Cardona and any associates."

People looked at one another. "Which one was he?" a young man, one of the group in knee britches, asked.

Rowley spoke up. "He was the fellow who asked about the casino during the bus tour. An older fellow, stocky. Dark hair. Wore a Panama hat. Those two came with him."

He pointed at Chago Aldama and the man next to him. Cornelia remembered that he was named 'Sal' something.

Chago scowled. "Hey, we had nothing to do with it."

"But you did arrive with him, didn't you?" Sheriff Bowden said. "According to the hotel records, he was paying for your room."

"Yeah, but we were just business associates. Haven't seen him since we were talking about the land deal."

"Not true," Teddy murmured to Cornelia. "I remember a Benny at the private party we went to. I think he might have been one of the hosts."

"That's probably not something our man Chago wants them to know about," she whispered back.

"I think you're right."

Bowden broke in. "Ladies and gentlemen, if you remember seeing Mr. Cardona, especially during the last day or two, we need your information. Seeing him won't make you a suspect, but keeping secrets could. Andy here is the person you need to talk to. And please—if you rode down on the Mullet Express, or are staying at this hotel, please stay in town until you're cleared. I know most of you just came to look at the property, so we'll try to make it fast. Mr. Aldama, Mr. Borerro, I'm interviewing you now. Come along. Don't go anywhere, Rowley."

The professor turned to his niece. "It seems my visit to Saint Petersburg will be delayed."

"This has been an interesting day," Teddy said cheerily during their ride back to the Riverside Lodge. She wanted to change for the party in Chago's suite. Cornelia thought that if the Cuban and his friend were arrested, it would probably put a major damper on things. "Do you think Peter killed both of them?"

"Horsefeathers," Pettijohn replied. "Anyone on the train could have poisoned Janzen, most of them more easily than Rowley could've. He was in the other car. And since he's been here, he's been wheeling and dealing. Been in plain sight the whole time in multiple places."

Their chauffeur, the man with the stubble, tilted his head back slightly, but said nothing.

"But they'll use that against him," Teddy said. "It would be easier for him to get to his victims as a roving agent than, say, someone who stayed in one place all the time."

"I can think of another person who had an interest in Janzen, although I don't know what it is yet," Cornelia said.

"That big goon that tried to break into the professor's room?"

The driver took the next bend in the road more slowly than he had the previous evening.

"No, but I wouldn't be surprised if he were involved with Mr. Cardona's death. Someone who would attempt burglary isn't that far away from murder."

"Well, then, who else was interested in Janzen? Besides Mr. Hofstetter."

"Mrs.—" Cornelia realized that they had an audience. "Step on it and pay attention to the road, Mister, or I'll pin those big ears back on your head."

They traveled the rest of the way in silence. The river and their hotel soon loomed in the windshield.

"Cornelia, dear, I must impose on you to contact the Vinoy," the professor said. "I need this fellow to take me to a few other locations."

Cornelia was wary. "Such as?"

"The engineer's."

"Going to talk shop?"

"Among other things."

The movie that evening was "The Gold Rush", starring Charlie Chaplin. It was funny, yet sad at times. The Thanksgiving scene with the cooked boot reminded Cornelia of several lean years from her childhood. Still, the way Chaplin twirled the laces like spaghetti gave her a smile. How could he make tragedy so... funny? Beside her, Teddy giggled until she was in danger of another coughing fit.

Afterwards, they went directly to the private party. The mood was somber; Cardona was, in fact, the 'Benny' of the previous celebration. Shortly after their arrival in the suite's foyer, Chago's roommate exited one of the bedrooms. Other men were visible through the doorway, locked in conversation. The air around them was thick with smoke.

"Good evening, ladies." He gestured them away from the crowded bedroom into an equally crowded salon. "We'll be with you shortly. Some of Benny's friends just arrived. Hey, Charlie! Get a Mary Pickford for the lady here and a sidecar for her pal."

Cornelia bristled at being referred to as a 'pal', but the man was already gone. Teddy, meanwhile, strolled to the bar and awaited her drink.

After a moment, Cornelia joined her. "I don't like the mood here. Or those new men."

"No, there's definitely a storm brewing, but we weren't going to learn anything staying in our room."

"I'm worried about getting drenched if we stay here."

"Hey, how's tricks?"

Kathleen, wearing a dress with brilliant blue fringe, plunked down in the seat next to them. She carried a cocktail in one hand and a cigarette in the other.

Teddy was pleased. "Kathleen, dear! Did you enjoy the party last night?"

"I sure did! I was surprised to see you and your friend there. You dance really well."

Teddy fingered her beads. "Thank you. I've always loved dancing."

Kathleen took a puff. "I was worried when you pooped out. Was that the lung thing?"

70

"Yes, it was." She sighed. "The price I paid for serving in the War."

"You? You served in the Great War? What did you do?"

"Cornelia and I were nurses. We were stationed at one of the Army hospitals in France."

"Your families let you do that?"

Now, Teddy had to laugh. "We were hardly young ladies at the time. My grand running-away came much earlier."

"Really? You ran away?"

"I'm afraid my family had plans for me that didn't involve a career. I was of the generation when young ladies of good family were sent to finishing school as preparation for marriage."

Kathleen made a face and puffed again. "They still do that."

"Are you in finishing school? Where?"

"It doesn't matter. I was expelled."

Teddy's eyebrows lifted in delight. "Really?" She saw a bench and sat down. "Come here and tell me all about it, dear."

Cornelia left them to their gossip. The only things she knew about finishing school were ones she had learned from Teddy's stories. Growing up in Kentucky was a very different experience. She hadn't realized how different until Uncle Percival arranged for her to enter the nursing program at Johns Hopkins. Most of the other students had been city girls from the Northeast. None of them had ever baited a hook or hoed a field.

She drifted through the crowd listening to tidbits about the deceased and speculation of what had gotten him stuffed into that bin and iced down like a gutted fish. Unfortunately, no one made reference to Tiny Belluchi or one Percival Pettijohn.

When she returned to the bar, Kathleen was gone.

"Where did your friend go?" Cornelia asked. "Did she find a dancing partner?"

"No, she went back to the hotel. Her Aunt Helen set a curfew for her. Something about her drifting in at an unseemly hour last night."

"It's for the best," Cornelia said. "This place isn't exactly the best influence on a young girl."

"Too late for me, I'm afraid. I became thoroughly corrupt some decades ago." She finished her cocktail and set it on a nearby tray.

"I think you started that way."

"I think you may be right. Ah, look. Here comes Chago." The dark young man slipped through the crowd and joined them. Teddy reached out to touch his cheek. "Poor boy. I'm so sorry about your friend."

"Ladies," Chago said, "I'm glad you could brighten this sad occasion."

"Have the police learned anything?"

He chuckled, but did not smile. "They're not going to learn much at all, *Señorita* Teddy. The killers won't talk, and if I knew who they were, I wouldn't say. I'd take care of them myself."

"That would be very dangerous," Teddy said. "You mustn't." Then, a glint came into her eye. "Some men tried to break into the professor's room last night. I wonder if they were the same ones."

The glint was returned by a glimmer in Chago's own. "What men?"

"Last night. Cornelia woke everyone up. She heard voices and thought they wanted to break into her uncle's room."

Now his eyes, dark and intense, focused on Cornelia. "Tell me what happened."

She cast a resentful look at Teddy, then told Chago about the men. Comprehension dawned on his face, which was annoying since he didn't offer to share his revelations with her. How could last night's incident be connected to the death? Cardona wasn't even staying in their hotel.

Still, there was something they weren't being told.

The ride back to the Riverside Lodge that night was a foggy one. It was also exceptionally dark.

"How do you not get lost out here?" Teddy asked the chauffeur, slurring the words. Cornelia had suggested she cut

72

down on the Mary Pickfords at the party, and the response had been a switch to planter's punch. The driver was the same one they'd had earlier. His name was Mitch, and he had come up from Tampa to get the extra work.

"It's not that hard," Mitch told them. "There's really only one turn you have to make. After that, you just have to stay on the main drag till you get to whichever hotel you're headed for."

They heard a loud whistle just then.

"Oh, now I know you're lost," Teddy said. "That's the train station."

He leaned forward in his seat to look, puzzled. "Couldn't be. We passed it already. It's one of the few places out here that has a light next to it."

"Maybe you circled by accident."

"Can't do that, either. Even if I made a wrong turn, it'd just take me to a dead end or the river. Besides, the train only makes one run. At this time of night they're loading freight for tomorrow's run. Look, there's the hotel now."

The Lodge's lights glowed in the fog. Too many lights. The doors were open to accommodate the number of people awake and standing in the hallway.

"What the hell? 'Scuse my French, ladies."

"Uncle Percival," Cornelia cried, and she threw the door open. Mitch slammed on the brakes, and she was off, Teddy following more slowly with her cane's assistance.

The Carsons were standing on the patio. "What's happened? Has something happened to my uncle?" She shoved Mr. Carson aside to get a better view.

"I don't know," Rosemary said. "We were asleep, and then this horrible noise woke us up. I thought the train had jumped the tracks."

Kathleen waved her arm at Cornelia. "Come here! It's Teddy, Mr. Hoyt, and she's with the professor's niece. Maybe she knows something."

The crowd parted, and she stepped through gratefully. Teddy and Mitch were behind her now.

Her uncle stood in front of his door, a stubborn expression on his face. His face was red hot and his snow white beard bristled like the quills of a porcupine.

Mr. Hoyt was equally red-faced, under the dust and sand that covered his hair and shirt.

Pettijohn shook his finger at the night manager. "It's not my fault that you don't have a watchman. It was within my rights to take measures for my own safety."

"Oh, Good Lord," Cornelia said. "What have you done this time?"

"What do you mean, 'this time'?"

The manager turned. "Yeah, what does that mean, 'this time'?"

"You left us so you could meddle with something, didn't you? What did you do?"

"I merely created a safety alarm for the window. In case someone decided to force it, which is what happened." He glared at Hoyt. "You should have a man to patrol the grounds, or patrol them yourself."

Cornelia could have kicked herself for not seeing this scene coming. He'd told them he was going to visit the engineer. "You borrowed a whistle, didn't you? How'd you get it to work?"

Her uncle looked pleased with her guess. "I got some parts at the hardware and attached the horn to the steam radiator. It was rigged to blow if someone opened the window."

"It woke everyone up, ma'am," Hoyt added, wiping around his eyes with an already-filthy handkerchief.

"Of course it did! That was the point! There was a day when I would have dealt with a burglar myself, but that was on my own property."

Teddy whooped and began to laugh; Mitch grinned. Cornelia glared at them both until the chuckling stopped. Then she turned back to her uncle. "What did you do to him?" She pointed at the night manager.

"I did nothing to him. He came through the door unannounced and fell victim to his own haste."

"Uncle..."

"He'll be fine," the professor insisted. "A man has to protect himself. Besides, it's just a bump on the noggin and a bit of dirt. I procured a pail of gravel and sand and balanced it on the transom. It was set to fall if case someone came in through the door."

"I see that Mr. Hoyt did. Has anyone checked you for injury, sir?"

"Not yet." He rubbed his head and winced, then shook some of the sand out. "I probably have a concussion. When that steam horn sounded, I thought the train was coming through the wall. I entered his room to see what was up."

"I'm very sorry." Cornelia glared at Uncle Percival. "See? Setting traps keeps people from helping you, too."

"He should have said something before barging in."

"I did," Hoyt snarled, "at the top of my lungs!"

"My mistake. It took me a while to shut the whistle off and put on my hearing aid. You should have waited."

"No, he shouldn't have. There could have been something seriously wrong, Uncle."

Uncle Percival was impossible.

"Mr. Hoyt," Cornelia asked, "would it be possible for us to change rooms?"

"Not with us," Helen Minyard said. "Then we would be facing the burglar or enemies Professor Pettijohn has made. He says he's retired, but what if he had to retire for other reasons? Like—like gambling debts, or unseemly behavior?"

The old man bellowed with laughter. "Please go on! You make me sound so exciting."

Mrs. Minyard fumed.

Teddy palpated Hoyt's head, making him squirm. "Hold still. You have an impressive knot there, plus a laceration from the edge of the pail. A perfect arc. I'm surprised you didn't bleed more. Head wounds usually gush."

She checked his eyes.

"Pupils same size, appear normal. I suggest that you wash your hair as soon as possible. An ice pack should reduce the swelling, and please try to keep the wound clean. I'm sure you'll recover without incident, but you should see a doctor in the morning to be certain."

"See a doctor? Who's gonna pay for that?"

Cornelia answered. "My uncle will. It is his fault, after all."

"Yeah, it is. He's going to pay for that, and repairs to the room. After I speak to the owner, he may be paying for hotel rooms somewhere else, too! I don't care if he is some kind of famous inventor. Thomas Edison stayed here and wasn't nearly as much trouble as your uncle."

The manager stomped off.

The crowd began to disperse, now that the show was ending.

"Thrown out of our rooms," Teddy said. "I haven't been thrown out of a hotel since the War."

"You were thrown out of a hotel? What for?" Mitch asked.

"My still blew up. It started a fire."

Mitch snorted.

"You let it overheat. I warned you about that before I went to the *boulangerie*," Cornelia said.

Chapter 8

Tiny Belluchi was having a bad morning. He hadn't gotten any sleep the past couple of nights, sneaking around the Riverside Lodge with Cesare. Then Leo had kittens when they returned empty-handed the second time. He kept asking why Tiny didn't have the camera yet, when the owner was just an elderly man with a couple of old ladies trailing him. If they were normal people, stealing a camera from them would have been duck soup. There was nothing normal about the old gent. He was more trouble than any copper Tiny had ever dealt with. Too bad the boss wouldn't let him eliminate the problem in the usual way.

Leo didn't want to call down any more attention on their heads. They knew the heat would start when Cardona's bin got opened, but then that old geezer had shown up at just the wrong moment with one of those newfangled moving picture cameras. Sure, he'd been focused on the fishing operation that was finishing up down by the river, but there was a good chance that the lens had caught Tiny and Cesare when he turned to film the train pulling into the stationhouse.

They hadn't noticed him cranking his camera while they were loading Cardona's body into a bin and shoveling in layers of ice and fish. Tiny liked the new twist he'd added to 'sleep with the fishes', but up the line somewhere those fish were going to be unloaded. Sooner or later, the coppers would trace Cardona's body back to Homosassa. He needed to get that film and be long gone when that happened.

They'd tried the simple approach—burglary—but that hadn't worked. Those old ladies had good ears for their age, drunk or not, and Gramps booby-trapped the room the next night. Tiny had never heard a whistle that loud. Not even the Chicago Els made that much racket. He and Cesare had ripped their clothes running away through the trees. Then he tripped on a cactus and got a leg full of needles. Who knew that there were cacti that didn't grow in the desert?

The time for tiptoeing was over. The old guy never went anywhere without that camera. They were just going to have to follow him and take it from him by force. Tiny and Cesare would need to lie low for a while afterwards, but Leo said there were some new guys coming up from Tampa anyway. He kicked them out with orders not to return without the camera.

Now the pair were crouched behind a nearby stand of trees near the Riverside Lodge's patio, waiting for the old guy to finish his egg sandwich. Palm fronds poked the Italian's exposed neck. Where did this guy have to be at this time of the morning? It wasn't even light yet. Tiny's stomach rumbled; he'd grabbed an orange when he left the hotel, but that was all the food he'd had.

The geezer checked his watch and stood rapidly. He wrapped the remainder of the sandwich in a napkin, and stuffed it into his jacket pocket. Then, he gathered up his camera equipment and headed for the front of the hotel. Tiny and Cesare circled around with him, staying in the shadows.

A Cadillac pulled up to the entrance. The driver got out and approached the old man. He took the equipment and headed for the car's trunk. Tiny and his partner ran for the boiler they'd brought up from Tampa.

The Cadillac circled round and headed for the main road. The pair followed at a distance. The sky was lightening now, so they didn't need to turn on their headlamps.

It was a short trip. The Caddy stopped at the rail station and the driver exited again to help Gramps out. Tiny drove the Ford Roadster up one of the dirt trails and parked it as far back in the trees as it would go.

Mud squished under their shoes as they found their way back to the crushed limestone road. His mug had better be on that film, with all the crap he was taking. Cesare swatted something green and leggy off his sleeve.

Their mark was standing at the engine. The train guys were jawing with him like they were old pals. One of the railmen took the equipment from the trunk of the Cadillac and stowed it away in the front passenger car. Then, the old man got a boost up onto the engine.

"Is he gonna drive it or something?" Cesare whispered.

"Maybe he drove it during the Revolutionary War and wants to take it for a trip down Memory Lane. It's a rust bucket, that's for sure."

"Where ya think he's going?"

"I dunno, but I think we're taking a train ride."

The knock at the ladies' hotel room came in the late morning, but still far too early for Teddy. She pulled the pillow over her head. Cornelia threw her robe on and cracked the door.

An eye and a mustache, topped by a uniform hat, appeared in the narrow space. "Are you Miss Lawless or Miss Pettijohn?"

"Miss Pettijohn. May I assist you some way?" It was the sheriff. Alarm sprang from the depths of her belly, and she threw the door open. "Is it my uncle? Has something happened?" They shouldn't have left him alone last night. He'd been fine after the incident, but Belluchi could have forced his way in with a gun, and they wouldn't have heard. Especially Teddy, when she was in her cups.

Sheriff Bowden, startled, stepped back. "As far as I know, he's fine—and according to the staff here, quite capable of looking after himself. I need to speak to you ladies. Would you be kind enough to meet me on the patio in a few minutes?"

"Of course."

Cornelia poked Teddy. "The sheriff wants to talk to us."

A moan emanated from under the pillow. "Is it about my untimely death?"

"Yes."

"I'll still be dead this afternoon. Have the funeral home come pick me up at two."

"Teddy." She grabbed a hip and shook it. "Come on. He's waiting for us on the patio."

Her companion moaned again, but sat up. "Those evil police—no respect for the dearly departed."

Cornelia went to the bath and splashed her face with water. She dressed and returned to the room. Teddy was lying on the coverlet, half dressed. "Sleeping again? I don't believe it."

"Yes, you can," said the muffled voice from the pillow.

"Either you get up and finish dressing, Theodora Lawless, or no more parties for you. And I will commandeer your stash, and ration it out to you in the correct medical dose!"

"So cruel!" Teddy whined, but sat up.

Despite the delay, the sheriff was still waiting for them on the patio. A cup of coffee and an orange juice rested on the table in front of him.

"All the free juice you want, courtesy of the developers. You won't tell 'em I'm not buying, will you?"

Cornelia smiled slightly. "It will be our secret."

"You were worried about your uncle, ma'am, when I knocked on your door. Why do you fear for his safety?" Bowden asked.

She thought about lying, saying that she was just worried about her elderly uncle, but the situation had become serious. "Last night, someone tried to break into his room. It wasn't the first time."

"Tell me more. Let's get something to keep up our strength while you do it." Bowden waved at the waitress, who came over with coffee and juice on her tray.

Cornelia ordered ham and grits. The sheriff ordered eggs, sausage, biscuits, and a rasher of bacon.

Susie nodded and turned to Teddy. "Do you need an ice pack this morning, miss?" she inquired.

"No, thank you. I think the coffee will do. And some dry toast."

"Are you well, Miss Lawless?" the sheriff inquired. "I didn't mean to pull you from your sickbed."

"It's merely the Florida heat," Teddy said. "Hot weather gives me a headache in the morning."

He looked skeptical, especially since it was early February, but let the matter go. "Okay, tell me what's been going on. I heard about the disturbance last night, but I don't have many details."

"Night before last, we had a window cracked. Due to the heat." She glared at Teddy. "I got up later to close it, and overheard some men outside talking about getting into an old geezer's room."

"And you made an assumption."

"A well-founded one, since they tried it again last night."

He pulled his notebook from his jacket pocket. "I presume that they didn't get in, or I would have heard about it."

"No, they didn't." Safe in the light of day, speaking to this lawman, she could see some of the humor in the failed attempt. "Uncle Percival is a semi-retired engineer. He rigged an alarm to wake him up if they tried again. A loud one. Mr. Hoyt will probably tell you all about it if he's still on duty."

"It was loud, all right," said the waitress, back at tableside with their food. "I could hear it from my house down the street. I thought someone was trying to steal the train."

Bowden frowned. "What sort of alarm was this?"

She gave him a short explanation of the professor's expertise with steam-powered devices. The waitress laughed, and even the sheriff fought a smile.

"He sounds like quite a character. You should have contacted my office, though, the first night."

"I don't know what could have been done." She waited until Susie left again.

Bowden split a biscuit and made a sandwich with the sausage patty.

Teddy fanned herself with her napkin, turning chartreuse.

Cornelia brought the man's focus back to her. "Incidents that almost happened, but didn't, are a little difficult to investigate."

The sheriff stood up. "Indeed they are, ma'am. Equally hard are incidents that might have happened and might not have."

"Such as?"

"Excuse me for a moment, ladies." Bowden stalked off toward the river; for a while he just stood there with his shoulders squared, his back to them. He wheeled round and returned to the table. He looked resolute. "Yesterday, Deputy Davidson spoke to you about Mr. Janzen's death."

"Yes," Cornelia said. "We also noticed him giving Peter Rowley a hard time about it here yesterday."

"Rowley doesn't get along very well with Andy." The mustache curved over his upper lip, revealing a wry smile. "Looking over his report, I'd say that he asked you all the questions about the fight and later death that I would have asked."

Cornelia nodded, waiting for the other shoe to drop.

"Andy tells me that Mr. Janzen sat next to your uncle on the train during the trip down."

"Yes, he did. He didn't start there, but it was closer to the lavatory than the seat he originally had."

"So, you're saying he was already sick."

"Yes, of course. You would be better off asking my uncle these questions."

"I agree, Miss Pettijohn, but he seems to have made himself scarce. Do you know where he is?"

"No. I'm afraid he didn't tell us his plans before we went to sleep." Cornelia didn't like the idea that her uncle was missing. If the hotel had evicted him, wouldn't he have woken them up? "I thought, on the train, that Mr. Janzen was suffering from the blows Mr. Hofstetter dealt him. Have you interviewed Mr. Hofstetter?"

"Oh yes, Andy and I have both spoken to him. They had a real estate partnership in Miami that ended badly. I learned a few other things, too. Are you aware your uncle was suing Mr. Janzen?"

Teddy stopped fanning. "Really? What for?"

Bowden continued to stare at Cornelia, who felt sandbagged. "He didn't mention it to me. My uncle does sue people from time to time, though, generally for patent infringement." Why hadn't he told her about it, especially if the man he was suing had died?

The sheriff wiped his mouth and pulled out his notebook. "In this case, he was suing England Homes. That's based out of England, Arkansas, not the country. Mr. Janzen was the registered agent."

Cornelia immediately remembered Uncle Percival's ill-considered trip at Thanksgiving to visit an old student in Little Rock. The damp, cold trip by train was responsible for the pneumonia and resultant delicate health that had forced her to come to Florida with him in the first place.

Teddy filled in the lull of conversation. "Is that a construction company, or an architectural firm?"

"Neither, exactly. It was a business that sold mail-order houses—sort of like the ones they're putting up in Aladdin City right now. They just did a 'dawn-to-dusk' demonstration—built a house in one day from the kit."

Her eyebrows, smudged from the night before, lifted. "You can order a house in the mail?"

"Not everyone is born in an ancestral mansion like yours," Cornelia said. "Or on an old farmstead as I was, for that matter."

"The kit is a bunch of materials pre-cut from the company, the lumber and such," the sheriff said. "They ship it to the place you plan to build, and you put it up without having to hire a bunch of people. Great time and money saver. Sears and Roebuck do a brisk business with them."

"Aladdin City sounds more romantic," Teddy opined.

His mustache curved with his smile again. "Yes. Well. Anyway, Miss Pettijohn, your uncle was suing England Homes for fraud."

Cornelia's mind raced backward over the past three months. She'd just returned to her home in Fisher's Mill, where she planned to stay once she officially retired from the Army Nurse Corps. The farmhouse needed repairs and renovations, ones her uncle had been very helpful in arranging. Once the house was ready, Teddy came from Arizona. A lot of adjustments had to be made, especially as the climate disagreed with Teddy's health. In the middle of the fuss, Uncle Percival had taken it into his head to travel south. Now, he thought a winter home would be the ideal solution for him and possibly Teddy, too.

"He's done some barn design in the past for agricultural purposes, so I suppose home building could be a new interest. Did they steal one of his designs?"

"No, ma'am. He was a financial backer of the company. An investor. He charged them with taking money for manufacturing that was never done."

That sounded like the old goat. Why was she just learning this now? "They weren't constructing the kits?"

"According to the complaint, there wasn't even a factory. Says here that your uncle went to the legal address of the business and found an empty lot in the middle of the swamp. Lotta swamp up in Arkansas."

"At which point he filed suit. That makes sense."

"You said your uncle sued other people. What did he do in those cases?"

"He usually confirmed that someone was using a patented item or process of his without paying for it, then filed suit."

"Confirmed it. Did he confront the violator personally?"

"In court, yes. Sheriff Bowden, usually the violator was some company or other that either thought they could escape detection, or had a designer who'd hit upon the same idea by accident. He's a very clever man. The Stanley people even purchased the rights to some of his patents to prevent competition from other automobile companies."

"Companies. Not people."

"Companies are run by people, Sheriff. He occasionally named individuals in his suits, especially if he felt they'd tried to slip one past him. Uncle Percival worked hard for his money and has a sharp eye on where it is invested."

"He is thorough."

She nodded. "Yes."

"He was through in this case, too. According to Mr. Hofstetter, your uncle got the names of the other investors from the business filing in Little Rock and organized the suit.

Since the mail-order business was supposed to dovetail with the real estate operation in Miami he ran with Hofstetter, they started looking at that, too."

"You said it ended badly. I presume the suit is why?"

"Exactly. They were fending off requests from the authorities to examine their books, and their clients wanted their money back. Seems that Mr. Janzen emptied the bank account and took a powder. Hofstetter was left holding the bag, and an empty one at that."

"No wonder he punched him," Teddy said. She leaned towards Bowden, twirling her beads. "How did they both wind up here? Did Mr. Hofstetter track him down?"

"That's neither here nor there, ma'am. My question to you two is: did Percival Pettijohn track him down?"

Cornelia opened her mouth to say no, and then closed it again. She wasn't so sure any more. Her uncle was bull-headed enough to chase down a scoundrel who tried to put one over on him. Setting things right would be more important to him than the money.

"I don't know. When he was younger, he would have," she said, and sighed. "I was stationed in California until three months ago."

Once the sheriff had left, Cornelia sat and thought for a while. Teddy finished her toast and became brave enough to ask for a slice with butter.

"We need to find my uncle," Cornelia said.

"Maybe he's off taking pictures again."

"I hope it's that simple. He could be in the hands of Mr. Belluchi and his cohorts."

"He also could be trying to book us new rooms. It's getting hot around here, and I don't mean the weather."

"The climate has turned decidedly hostile," Cornelia agreed. "I do want to find him, though. He has designs going on that I didn't know about."

"Just because he's old doesn't mean he's not sneaky."

"Well, he's going to stop being sneaky with me. And after I beat the truth out of him, I need to speak to Mrs. Minyard," Cornelia said.

"About her visit to Mr. Janzen's room? It does sound rather apropos. Why didn't you tell the sheriff about her?"

"Because she didn't walk out with anything that looked like luggage. I wanted to ask her why she was there before I spoke to anyone. Why didn't you bring it up?"

"Because I was afraid if I spoke too much, I would spew. Especially when I could smell that sausage."

"Damn that Florida heat. In February."

"I am a delicate flower."

Cornelia rolled her eyes at that line. Aside from her damaged lungs, there was nothing frail about Theodora Lawless.

"You might be a less delicate flower if you weren't potted every night."

Teddy tried to look offended, but broke into a grin.

"How you go on," she said.

Tiny Belluchi and his cohort rode in the first passenger car. They tried getting close to the gear stowed in the front, but the conductor was having none of that. If it had just been the three of them, Tiny would have played a little chin music with him, but there were a lot more customers on the train than this backwater burg deserved. It wasn't a real town yet. He glanced out the window, spotting a chain gang of saps working on what they called a road here. It wasn't even paved, for Chrissake.

After about twenty minutes, the train pulled into another small station. The schedule listed it as a mail drop, but a couple of railmen came for the old geezer's equipment. Tiny elbowed Cesare, who was snoring next to him.

"Looks like this is our stop."

"But we're paid all the way to Ocala," his sleepy partner muttered.

"Maybe another day. C'mon." Tiny could see the white-haired man already standing on the platform, talking to the fireman through the open locomotive window.

The conductor made a token objection to their disembarking, but let them go. Tiny thought he was happy to see the back of them; suits and fedoras were viewed with suspicion in these parts. Suits with a bulge under the left arm, anyway.

Another car was waiting outside the station. The old man walked right up to it and got in, leaving his tripod for the driver to handle. Tiny ran towards it, waving his arms.

"Hey, buddy! Can we share your ride? I got money!"

No use; the car was already pulling out, leaving a spray of pebbles in its wake.

"What now?" Cesare asked.

"We get a hack and find him. How much town could there be here? It wasn't even a real stop."

It took a while for Tiny and his buddy to get a ride. Wasn't a proper cab, just a local fellow who would take them around in his bucket for a couple of dollars.

The lanky local looked the pair up and down. He wore a short-sleeved shirt and pants with suspenders. Tiny realized that their suits would make them conspicuous.

"You boys looking to buy some prop'ty here in town?" the yokel asked.

"Yeah, maybe. Lots of buyers comin' by?"

"Nah, most of 'em are goin' further south. We have a lot to offer, though—gas station, good fishin', close to the county seat. Even got our own police station." He pointed to a squarish building near the bank. "Safe place."

Both men instinctively sank lower in their seats, somewhat ineffectively in Tiny's case. "Yeah, I see that," Belluchi said. "Say, you want to take us somewhere else? Maybe somewhere more scenic." He hadn't noticed Gramps filming many city buildings.

"What sort of scenic? Trees? Fishing?"

"Fishing, yeah. Maybe with alligators. People like to take pictures of those."

"Okay, here we go," their driver said, and made a U-turn. "But I wouldn't do any close shots if I were you."

After the almost unbearable breakfast, Teddy went back to the room and collapsed. Her cough woke her. The sunlight was brilliant enough to make her wince, and she wished she had pulled the shades before going to sleep. She lifted the pillow from her head and fumbled in her bag for her medicine flask. "Hair of the dog," she said to no one in particular. Judging from her headache, she was going to have to break open a new bottle before the day was over. For a long time she lay in bed, her head buried under the pillow again, as she pieced together the fragments of memory. Chago's party, the alarm, poor Mr. Hoyt. His head must ache almost as bad as hers this morning. That bucket gave him quite a whack.

Her hand drifted to the edge of the bed. Cornelia was a grouch, and she snored like an old bear, but not finding the familiar lump curled in the bed beside her gave her a moment of panic. Teddy willed herself to calm down. Cornelia hadn't adjusted to civilian life. She was up at the crack of dawn every morning. *Probably off birdwatching again with that Carson woman.*

Teddy lifted the pillow and opened one bloodshot eye. The sun was awfully bright. How late was it, anyway?

With everyone else out taking advantage of the West Coast Company's hospitality, this was a good time to have a long soak in the bath. She was more than happy to skip the sales pitches in favor of some old-fashioned pampering.

Cornelia was sitting on the edge of the bed looking at a magazine when Teddy emerged from the bath. A hobo with a bindle stood on the cover, blocking part of *The Saturday Evening Post*'s title.

"Glad to see you're alive," Cornelia said.

"No thanks to you. How could you abandon me in my hour of need?"

"It is nearly noon, and you haven't dressed yet. I imagine you were happily snoring for several hours after I left."

"Yes, I was," Teddy replied. "So what have you been up to this morning?"

Cornelia smiled. "Rosemary and I took a johnboat through the salt marsh this morning. It was really beautiful with the sun coming up over the water and turning the black spikes of marshgrass to shades of brown and green."

"It's Rosemary now. Not Mrs. Carson? What does her husband think of that?"

"Theodora, are you jealous? She's a married woman with two children."

"Well?"

Cornelia chuckled, and her blue eyes crinkled at the corners. She picked up the dress Teddy had laid out on the bed and tossed it to her. "Get dressed, you little goose. We're going to go to the grand hotel to plan a party for Uncle."

Teddy brightened and gathered her things.

The yokel was true to his word. Within five minutes, they were in the middle of nowhere, staring at a river of dark green water. Unfortunately, there was no sign of the geezer they were tracking.

"You call this scenic? Reminds me of the alley behind my ma's apartment. Muddy and wet."

"I didn't know they had pines in Florida," Cesare said, and got another elbow.

"Muddy and wet is what gators like," the driver said.

"I don't see no gators."

"They don't want you to see 'em. See those logs out there?"

Tiny squinted. "Yeah."

"Only two of them are logs. The third one is a gator looking for lunch."

"Looking for a nap, more like. Take us somewhere else scenic."

They drove around until Cesare spotted the car the old man had gotten into. And there he was, perched at the edge of the water, grinding away at that camera.

Tiny followed Cesare's pointed finger. "Here. Here is scenic. Slow down."

"Okay," The yokel hit the brake. "Don't know what the difference is, but you fellas are the ones paying for the view."

"Why don'tcha park over here?" 'Here' was a small break in the trees, not far from Gramps but hidden from view. "My pal and I are going to get out. Enjoy the scenery. Don't you leave, or there'll be hell to pay."

"Gotcha."

Tiny got out of the car and unkinked his legs, which still smarted from the cactus thorns. Too many dirt and crushed-rock roads. Didn't anyone down here believe in pavement? He wiped his neck, already damp from the humidity.

The old man bent over his equipment, heedless of their approach. The fella he was using as a driver was still at the car, studying a map. He wasn't close enough to interfere if they just strolled up and did a snatch-and-run. The yokel they'd come with might kick about being the getaway driver, but Tiny had a convincer under his jacket that should shut him up quick.

He gestured for Cesare to flank their prey from the other side, then reached under his arm to ease the gun out. The sound of a motor behind him made him freeze in place.

A car with the emblem of the sheriff's department passed the two Italians, coming to a stop behind the old geezer's ride. A young guy—not the sheriff—exited the vehicle and headed for the river. Tiny and his friend made for the trees.

"Jeez," Cesare muttered, once they were shielded by palm fronds. "Ya think they followed us?"

"Couldn't be. But maybe they figger he saw somethin'."

"Like what?" a voice asked behind them.

It was the yokel. He stared beyond them at the two cars by the river. "Huh. That's the deputy that lives in Homosassa. Wonder what he wants?"

Tiny didn't want to create a scene, especially a noisy one, so he didn't belt the guy for following them. "Maybe he likes to fish during his lunch break."

"Naw, looks like he's talkin' to those fellas."

The trio watched as the deputy spoke to the old man, who became agitated with whatever the subject matter was. After a few minutes, the deputy escorted their mark to the back seat of his car. He and the other driver gathered up the photography equipment and put it in the trunk of the sheriff's vehicle. Both cars left.

"Sheesh," Cesare said. "They nabbed him."

"Maybe he didn't have a permit," the yokel said. "Anyway, you've got more scenery to enjoy now."

90

"Ain't that just peachy." Leo was going to kill them both when they got back to the hotel. Why couldn't he have just let Tiny shoot the old geezer?

Chapter 9

Once the party arrangements were made, Cornelia and Teddy
went in search of their errant traveling companion. Rosemary
Carson and her husband came into the hotel as they entered
the lobby. She smiled when she spotted Cornelia.

"My dear, you should have been with us this morning.
There was a bald eagle with talons as big as my fist. He
swooped down and snatched a fish right out of the river. It was
thrilling."

"It certainly sounds so," Cornelia said. "I'd much rather
be pursuing a bird of prey than the old buzzard I'm chasing. By
any chance, have you seen my uncle?"

Mrs. Carson tried not to giggle.

"Not since he woke us last night. He seems to be more
of a handful than both my children together. I don't envy you
the task of keeping up with him."

"He left early this morning," her husband said. "I was
out on the patio having a smoke when the old gentleman came
out carrying his motion picture camera. He got into one of the
company cars. That is your uncle, right?"

Cornelia shook her head.

"Did you see which way he went?"

"Toward town. He's probably just shooting more of his
film."

He put an arm around Rosemary. "I have to agree with
my wife. At eight-and-a-half and five, our children are a
handful, but I would rather have them at their worst than keep
up with your uncle."

"I would have to agree," Sheriff Bowden said, joining
the four of them. "I haven't met the Carson children, but your

uncle is more trouble than a whole passel of young'uns. I've had to lock him up as a material witness—although, really, more for flagrant disregard of my orders."

Cornelia tried not to gape. "What?"

"Professor Pettijohn hopped the morning train and disembarked before it reached its final destination. Then, he hired a private driver who could have taken him anywhere, and loaded what looked like a suitcase into the trunk. Andy had the local authorities hold him."

She could barely breathe. "Where is he being held?"

"In the Crystal River Jail. He is a likable enough fellow, and seems like an educated man. What part of 'please stay put until you're cleared' do you reckon he failed to understand?"

"Crystal River isn't that far. Maybe he forgot about your request."

Incredulity crossed Sheriff Bowden's face.

"Miss Pettijohn, I've interviewed the professor at length. He is not a man who forgets anything. Yet, he didn't see fit to tell me that he was suing Mr. Janzen. In combination with his actions today, that's very suspicious behavior."

Cornelia tried to keep the worry out of her face. He hadn't seen fit to tell her he was suing Janzen, either. Still, with all the contracts for his inventions, he might not know the particulars of every case. No, she was making excuses. Deep down, she knew the sheriff was right about her uncle's memory. Uncle Percival's body was frail, but his mind was as sharp as ever. If the sheriff wanted to know when she had lost her first baby tooth, Uncle Percival could probably tell him to the exact moment it happened. He remembered every detail of everything he saw.

"Can we see him?" she asked.

"Of course, I was coming to fetch you. We can go now if you would like."

When Cornelia and Teddy saw Uncle Percival, it was in the city jail of Crystal River. The sheriff, who had given them a ride, escorted them out of the car and into the small building constructed of stone blocks. It couldn't have contained more than three rooms.

"This is some way to spend a birthday," Cornelia muttered.

The sheriff nodded to the jailer and walked toward a wooden door on the left. Cornelia tried to follow him, but Davidson blocked her path.

"I'm sorry, ma'am, but the sheriff needs to speak with him first. In private."

"You can't talk to my uncle without an attorney present!" Cornelia shouted at Bowden's back. "I demand to know what you intend to do with him."

The sheriff stopped and turned. "Miss Pettijohn, all we want to do right now is ask him some questions. From what you told me earlier, he's quite familiar with our legal system. Right now, though, he's not formally under arrest. He's a suspect who skipped town."

"Skipped town?"

"Everyone was asked not to leave Homosassa, ma'am. Not even to go sightseeing in another town."

"That was because of Mr. Cardona, though—not Mr. Janzen," Teddy protested.

"A distinction I'm sure he regrets now."

The ladies missed lunch. Cornelia spent the time fuming while Teddy chatted up the jailer. Percival Pettijohn was being held overnight as a convenience to Sheriff Bowden. After that, the sheriff might release him or, alternately, have him transferred to Inverness, the county seat.

What were they supposed to do if her uncle were formally charged with the murder? Would his attorney be willing to travel so far, even for a client that kept him on a hefty retainer?

The jail's interior felt like a cave, despite the front windows. Cool and clammy. She was certain there were no windows in the holding area. What effect would it have on her uncle's lungs? What if the pneumonia returned?

Two hours passed before the sheriff and his deputy left, allowing Cornelia and Teddy to enter the room. Instead of cells, there were cages from wall to wall. The old man sat on a cot inside a cage that was barely his own height, leaving him to face Cornelia's wrath without an escape route. Seeing his misery only made her angrier. This could have all been avoided if he'd confided in her.

Once they were alone, the irate niece confronted her dissembling uncle. "We had a fine interview with the sheriff this morning. You were in the process of suing Mr. Janzen, and didn't see fit to tell either of us."

"It didn't seem relevant when I was planning the trip. I intended to tell you before actually meeting with the gentleman. I use that term loosely. My research indicates that he has been involved in a number of shady deals."

"Is that why we made this trip?"

"Not entirely," the professor said, tapping the bars with the tip of one shoe. "I didn't mislead you about wanting to look into the Floridian climate for its health benefits."

"Since the air in Arkansas didn't agree with you?"

He sighed. "Corny, I'm used to handling my own financial affairs. Unfortunately, it seems that my health is not quite what it used to be."

"Don't call me Corny. Why didn't you stay home and let your attorney handle this?"

"Why shouldn't I call you Corny? You're just like your father, only with longer hair and a shorter temper!" the old man sputtered.

Teddy stifled a giggle behind Cornelia. She ignored it. "What did you hope to accomplish by coming here?"

"I wanted to confront the scoundrel myself," Pettijohn said. "I wanted to let him know that he wouldn't get away with swindling a Pettijohn. Once I settled that account, I planned to warn others of his scurrilous business practices. Your Grandfather Pettijohn would have challenged him to a duel, but modern law frowns on that. I've had to fight my battles through our somewhat flawed justice system."

Cornelia took in a long breath, then released it. "I can see where you would want to fight your own battles, but I wish you'd given us more warning of your real purpose in coming to this land sale."

"I intended to discuss it with you eventually, but the man managed to get himself into a world of hurt before we even arrived in Homosassa."

"Eventually, eh? The sheriff knows that he sat next to you on the train."

"Yes, which was a source of curiosity to him. Especially combined with the lawsuit."

"What did happen during that ride?"

Her uncle shook his head. "Not much. It was clear that Janzen didn't know who I was."

"What did he say?"

"Mostly, 'excuse me'. He was having a bad time."

"You didn't talk to him about his swindle at all?"

"Didn't have the chance. Every time I tried to strike up a conversation, he'd clutch his stomach and run to the lavatory."

They were both silent for a moment. Teddy jumped in. "So, what did the sheriff say when you told him that?"

"He didn't say much. He was mostly angry that I went to Crystal River to film some different scenery. As if I knew that he wanted to question me!"

"His view of your behavior is dim. I wish you'd let us know where you were," Cornelia said.

"I didn't want to wake you. I knew you'd had a long night, and that Teddy, at least, wouldn't be getting up any time soon."

Teddy stuck out her tongue.

The old man managed a smile. "Cornelia, it's already done and over. Since you have been kind enough to visit me during my captivity, could I persuade you to bring me some pajamas and a change of clothing? The jailer has my key. Perhaps Mitch would be kind enough to transport you. I think he finds us amusing."

"I bet he does. Are there any new booby traps I should watch out for?"

"Just the bucket."

"The bucket? But how did you get out of the room?" Teddy asked.

"I held the transom up with my cane and slid through. Just open the door slowly and have Cornelia use yours."

"He'd rather that I get conked than you," Cornelia said.

"You have a harder head, dear."

"Not as hard as yours. Next time you go off on a jaunt, please slide a note under the door to our room," Cornelia said.

"It won't be necessary. As per the orders of the Citrus County Sheriff's Office, if, and only if I am released, I am not to leave town again until I am cleared of suspicion. The news should confirm all of Mrs. Minyard's theories."

Mrs. Minyard. Now Cornelia truly needed to speak to her.

Tiny was glad he was talking to Leo on the telephone instead of in person. The boss was furious when he got Tiny's news. Giving them the slip was one thing, but letting the cops nab him and take the camera? Tiny hoped the operator wasn't listening in. She probably didn't understand Italian, but curse words seemed to be universally identifiable.

He held the receiver about a foot from his ear. Listening while he waited for Leo to take a breath. "Boss, we'll make it right. On my grandmother's grave."

Cesare, who was supposed to be keeping the yokel from overhearing the call, tugged his sleeve. "Hey, I gotta idea. He can't have all his film with him. Gramps' room is gonna be empty for sure."

"*Basta*! Not you, boss. There's a chance the particular goods might be back in his room. He's filmed a lot of palm trees."

The driver perked up and Tiny signaled Cesare to get back to the car.

"Yeah, yeah. Don't worry boss. We'll have it in your hands tonight," Tiny promised.

He hung up and walked back to the yokel's car. "Good news. It's almost quittin' time. You're taking us back to the train station. And there's an extra fin in it for ya if you keep your mouth shut."

Cesare said, "Couldn't he just take us all the way back? It'd be faster."

98

It was a tempting proposition. The Mullet Express was a rickety old tin can that lacked fans or padded seats. Tiny eyed the lanky man who'd been their driver. "Nah, this pitcher has long ears. I'd have to pin 'em back if we did that."

"Right."

The yokel finally looked disturbed. He'd gotten the message but good.

"What was that location again, ma'am?"

"The jail in Crystal River. Do you know where it is?"

"Yes, we do." The concierge for the West Coast Development Company was quite courteous and managed to keep most of the curiosity out of his voice. Cornelia appreciated it.

The concierge assured them that Mitch would be dispatched immediately. In fact, the man allowed, Mitch had taken a liking to the Pettijohns, and said he would be happy to drive them anywhere they needed to go. They must be a charming family.

Their uncle was right; Mitch did find them amusing. She hoped that nosiness was the reason and nothing more. Cornelia hung up the phone and thanked the jailer for its use. "We're leaving, but we will be back as soon as we can with some personal items for my uncle. Nothing dangerous, just some pajamas and fresh clothing."

"Does he use a denture cup? You might want to bring it if he does."

"No, but thank you for being so thoughtful. Is the jail heated at night?"

The man laughed, and she saw he was missing a few teeth of his own. "Cold ain't usually the problem here. If it gets chilly, though, the night man lights a fire. He has rheumatism."

Cornelia made a mental note to bring extra socks and his heavy robe.

Mitch arrived and helped them into his Cadillac. "Just the two of you?"

"Yes, just us."

Cornelia pressed her lips together until they disappeared. Why couldn't he just take them back to the Lodge? She needed quiet to gather her thoughts.

"Is your uncle staying here? What did he do?" His questions fired one after another.

"Never you mind," Cornelia snapped. "We need to return to the hotel and get some things for him. I hear you always have time for us, so I expect you're free to bring us back here."

"Yes, ma'am."

As they pulled onto the main road, Cornelia saw another chain gang of men painting what appeared to be a school. She tried not to picture her uncle among them.

It was getting on to dusk by the time they arrived in Homosassa. The deeper they went into town and its canopy of palms and live oaks, the darker it got. Mitch put the headlamps on, but they were of little use this time of day.

They had to slow as they got close to the river. Cars lined up in front of the Riverside Lodge to transport the guests to tonight's moving picture show at the Homosassa Hotel. The lights that had been of little use in seeing the road glittered off the sequins and spangles of the women's party gowns.

A pang of guilt tugged at Cornelia's emotions as Teddy's forlorn expression reflected back to her from the window. They hadn't even eaten since breakfast. Instead of laughter and good company, they were playing nursemaid to her uncle. Cornelia turned to Teddy.

"You don't have to go back with me, you know," she said. "Once we get my uncle's things together, you could stay behind and have some dinner. Or go to the party—I know you love them. Uncle Percival managed to turn the surprise on us, but that shouldn't stop you from greeting the guests. If I need help carrying Uncle Percival's things, Mitch can help me."

"No," Teddy said. "I'm not leaving you and the professor in the lurch. I might get my tin of Oreos out of our room, though."

Mitch turned in his seat. "There's a couple of places in town you could get a sandwich. Nothing fancy, but it's quick.

You could get something for the old guy, too. I don't know what they feed 'em in jail up here, but it's probably not what he's used to."

The suggestion made remarkable sense. "That's a good idea. Let's get what Uncle Percival needs out of his room, then see about some dinner."

"I think I still want those Oreos," Teddy said. "And I could get the Gertrude Stein book for the professor. It should take his mind off his circumstances."

"I think jail might be preferable."

Mitch went in with them, ostensibly to help them carry anything heavy. Maybe he was just being helpful, but Cornelia wasn't so sure.

When they reached the door to their room, Cornelia turned to him. "You stay here. I don't want you seeing any of our unmentionables."

The man grinned and nodded. He was beginning to get his evening stubble again. A man like him should shave twice a day, she thought.

Once they were in the room, Cornelia went to the nightstand. She gave Teddy the cookies and the book, then took the Colt M1911 out of the drawer. She put it in her leather bag and left the top unlatched. She wouldn't take it into the jail, but if their eager driver was more than he seemed, she wanted to be prepared.

"Do you think we have time to change clothing?" Teddy asked. "It's been a hot day."

Cornelia did not want to sit through another long session of makeup and hose-smoothing. "I think not. When we get back, though, baths are in order for both of us. I'm sure I smell like an infantryman after a ten mile hike by now."

They emerged from the room. Mitch was leaning against the wall watching their door.

"Thank you for waiting. Give him your cane, Teddy," she said, as they approached the professor's room. "I'm going to unlock Uncle Percival's door, and then you, Mr.—"

"Grant," Mitch said, taking the cherrywood cane.

"Mr. Grant will open it slowly." She pointed to the transom. "Can you see the bottom of the bucket balanced above the door? When you open the door, use the cane to keep it from falling while we slide through."

"And if it slips, be sure to jump back," Teddy added. "It leaves a painful bruise on the head."

"Just don't stand behind me," he said, and began easing it open. "And there it is."

"Okay, just prop it up while we—"

But Mitch had other plans. He pushed the transom up and the door forward at the same time, and the bucket dropped neatly into his hands. Teddy's cane clattered on the hardwood floor.

"That was very clever," Teddy said, retrieving her accessory. "If only Mr. Hoyt had been so quick."

Mitch set the bucket down near the door. "Do you want me to try putting it back up before we leave?"

"No, Mr. Grant, with everything that's going on, one of us is liable to forget at the wrong time. Besides, he's in a safe place at the moment." Cornelia emptied one of her uncle's smaller cases and set it on the bed. "Find his heaviest robe, Teddy. It may have to double as a blanket if the night is cool."

Teddy handed Mitch the book. He studied its contents, frowning, while she explored the wardrobe. "His jackets are in here, too. What color shirt are you packing?"

"Just grab one. It doesn't matter."

"Yes, it does." The clack of clothes hangers vied with her voice. "Your uncle is rather the peacock. You should see the suit he wears to University of Kentucky sporting events, Mitch. Brilliant blue broadcloth and a cane with the head of a wildcat."

Their driver chuckled. "I've seen it. He's a real character."

"I wish I could blame his erratic behavior on his age," Cornelia said, "but Uncle has always been irascible. It is humiliating to be reduced to searching his room to find out what other trouble he might be in."

"I like the old guy, and would like to help," Mitch said. "Why won't you tell me what he's gotten himself into?"

Cornelia rifled through the night stand and checked under the pillows on his bed to see if he'd hidden any other incriminating secrets in his room. She was about to confide her fears to the driver when the door burst open, and the man she'd identified as Tiny Belluchi came charging through shoulder first. He promptly fell over the bucket of sand and landed on his knees.

Cornelia's hand snaked into her purse, grasping the Colt, but Tiny's buddy already had his gun out.

"Everyone stay where you are," Cesare demanded

She froze, hand clasped around the butt of the gun. Drawing herself to her full height, she fixed the man with her sternest gaze. "You have no business in this room. Leave now, and I won't have to call the police." Her finger slid forward under the dark leather, curled around the trigger.

"Too late for that, Granny." Tiny stood again, towering over both her and Mitch. Teddy had seemingly vanished. She glared at the enormous thug, willing her eyes not to move to the wardrobe and its now-closed door.

"My uncle isn't here. What do you want with him?"

"None of yer business." He indicated Mitch. "Who's he?"

"My bodyguard," Cornelia stated boldly. "There are beasts in this jungle."

"Really? Looks like he needs glasses for that big book."

"It'll take more than glasses to understand this thing." Mitch said. "Look, fellas, the old guy's not here. Why don't you just skedaddle before someone gets hurt?"

"You're coming in on this late, pal." He turned back to Cornelia. "Where's the old geezer's camera?"

Cornelia smirked. "With the police. You're also a little late for that, sir."

"Where's his film?"

"In the camera, you fool."

"Don't play dumb with me. He's got more film than that. Thinks he's a regular D.W. Griffith, all the time he's spent grinding that camera. Look in there." He gestured to the wardrobe. "Bet he has a case of the stuff. Get it for me and I might let you live."

Cornelia hesitated, and the man behind Tiny jerked his gun. "Now, you old bat!"

There was no choice. She half-opened the cedar doors and saw Teddy crouched there, holding the case up for her. Cornelia took it and handed her the purse.

"Is this what you want?" She lifted the leather film case.

"Open it up. Show me what's inside. I wasn't born yesterday."

"Neither was I." She flung the bag at him and ducked down. "Teddy, now!"

The cedar doors popped apart and Teddy fired a shot in the direction of the invaders. The bullet buried itself in the plaster as they scurried out of the way.

Mitch hurled the Gertrude Stein book at Cesare. It hit him in the eye. Cesare howled and backed towards the door to the hall, still clutching the gun.

"You should be ashamed, attacking a couple of women." Teddy shrieked, firing again. Tiny clutched his arm and fled through the door, followed by Cesare.

"Follow them," Cornelia shouted. "They've got the film."

"Lady, your uncle can buy more film. Those men are gangsters."

Cornelia pushed past him and out the door.

"There must be some evidence on it that would clear Uncle Percival. Otherwise, they wouldn't want it."

Teddy and Mitch bolted after her.

They took the path to the car so fast that Teddy started gasping for air.

Mitch saw her begin to swoon and swept her into his arms without breaking stride. He carried her the rest of the way to the car and settled her into the back seat.

"Look ladies," he said, as he turned the Cadillac around, sending a spray of gravel toward the river. "I'm not just a driver. I'm a reporter for the *Saint Petersburg Times*, working on a big story involving mob money and the proposed casino. Those guys we're chasing and their friend are part of Ignacio Antinori's gang. They came to Tampa by way of Chicago."

"Is that so?"

Mitch glared at Cornelia and nearly missed a curve.

"Watch the road," Teddy shouted.

Mitch jerked the wheel, narrowly missing a large palmetto palm, and pulled back onto the gravel road. By then, the flivver had put some distance between it and Mitch's car.

"Don't worry, ladies, it's all dead ends till we reach the road for the hotel. We're not going to lose them."

He stepped on the gas and the Cadillac lunged forward, closing the gap.

Cornelia rolled down the window.

"Teddy, hand me my gun. A little closer and I'll try to shoot out their tires."

"Mine's in the glove box," Mitch said, "along with a box of shells."

She opened the door in the dash and found a respectable .44 inside. It resembled her gun; perhaps Mitch had been a doughboy in his youth. She clicked the safety off and aimed. Just as she fired, the car hit a rut in the dirt road, causing her shot to take out the right taillight instead of their tire. She swallowed her curse.

"You were saying that we have a bunch of Chicago mobsters trying to get control of the new casino. Where does your newspaper come into this?"

"This bunch moved in on the Tampa rackets. Charlie Wall is also vying for the casino. The men your friend in the back has been partying with are Charlie's boys. Charlie's a home-grown crook who practically runs the Cuban district. He controls gambling, booze, and prostitution from Tampa. He considers all of Central Florida his territory and isn't about to let the Chicago mob move in."

"We're in the middle of a mob war," Teddy said between wheezes. "How exciting."

"This is the kind of excitement that gets people killed," Mitch replied. "If your uncle is tangled up with any of these men, he's in a lot bigger trouble than the local police or you ladies can handle."

The lone taillight ahead of them veered to the right and Mitch followed. Suddenly, it disappeared and the headlamps were bearing down on them.

"Cripes!" Mitch jerked the wheel hard to the right and they narrowly missed being sideswiped by the mobsters' car.

Cornelia saw the reason why the men had doubled back. Traffic was at a standstill on the road to the hotel. Both lanes were filled with lines of cars headed one way.

She thumped the side of the Caddy. "What the heck is going on tonight besides a busted birthday party?"

"Valentino movie," Teddy answered from the back. "Double feature."

Mitch got the car turned around on the narrow road as gracefully as an elephant in a cave. He followed the Ford's dust trail away from the hotel lights.

"They must not know where they're headed. The road ends at the river."

"Good," Cornelia said. They can't get away."

Once the gangsters crossed the bridge near the sporting lodge, they must have realized the same thing. The junker wheeled back toward the Cadillac, Tiny and Cesare firing from both sides of the car. In the middle of the bridge, the car turned sideways. The driver kept shooting while his bigger companion got out.

Mitch pulled to the side of the road and looked at Cornelia.

"What now?"

They watched as Tiny lifted a large rock from the side of the road and dropped it into the professor's film bag. He shot a couple of holes in the bag, tossed it into the river, then gave them a one finger salute before getting back in the car. Its wheels kicked up gravel as Cesare put it into gear.

Cornelia was a kettle boiling with rage.

"Ram them," she shouted.

"Look, lady, I don't own this car. It's time to go to the police."

Chapter 10

The Lodge had all lights burning when they returned. Mr. Hoyt stood in the doorway with Deputy Andy. Mitch began looking for a place to park the Cadillac.

"We're in for it now," Teddy said.

"We're not the only ones," Cornelia growled. "If these men were doing their proper jobs, criminals would not be breaking into hotel rooms at will and Uncle Percival would not be spending his birthday in jail."

"You have to forgive them," Mitch said. "The county probably hired a number of officers sufficient to handle the listed population on the last census. The last few years have been hell—excuse my French—everywhere there's a beach down here. Land speculators, new houses and citizens, plus an enormous number of tourists have been pouring in, and the crime has followed."

"West Coast should have provided extra security for their customers, then."

"You'd think they could afford it. They bought the land here for two bucks an acre." He inched the car up against a cabbage palm. "This is as close as we're going to get, ladies."

Teddy climbed out of the back. "I hope you don't have to sweep me off my feet again, Mitch, even though it was exciting."

The Lodge's porch was crowded with whispering guests. When they finally reached the entry stairs, the waiting men barraged them with questions and demands. Cornelia tried to answer the deputy first, but the overwrought Mr. Hoyt drowned her out.

She put two fingers in her mouth and whistled loudly. "Everyone shut up!"

Everyone shut up abruptly, and she nodded. "I think we should continue this in private. Quieter, and fewer people to overhear and gossip later."

"Let's use the office," Mr. Hoyt said. He led them to a small room filled to the brim with desk and files. "I'm sorry; I don't think I can fit enough seats for everyone in here."

"We can stand," Andy said.

"Miss Teddy should sit. She has some health problems." Mitch grabbed a chair from a nearby room and shoved the men aside. He planted it on the other side of the desk.

"How sweet." Teddy sat and balanced her cane between her feet and hands.

"Can we shut the door now?" Cornelia asked.

"If we all hold our breath for a moment," Andy said. They squeezed together, and the door was able to close.

"Now," Andy said. "Tell us what happened."

"We came back to get some pajamas and fresh clothing for my uncle," Cornelia said. "Since he has none where he is. While we were gathering them, two men burst in on us."

"Who were these men?"

"The large one was a Mr. Martino Belluchi. He's staying at the Homosassa Hotel. His companions are Cesare Ricci and Leonardo Mazzi. I believe it was Mr. Ricci who accompanied him. It wasn't Mr. Mazzi; I met him at one of the hotel soirees."

"You know them."

"Only through their attempts to break into my uncle's room. They've tried twice before, with very little protection from the management."

"You didn't tell me their names," Mr. Hoyt said. "That might have helped."

"I didn't know their names until recently. I learned who they were by looking into the matter myself."

"Ma'am, you should have told me or the sheriff," Andy said. "That's our job. Trying to investigate on your own was only asking for trouble."

Her face felt warm, and not just because of the close quarters. "I did tell the sheriff. The next time I saw him, he'd had my uncle arrested."

"Arrested?" Hoyt squeaked. "For what?"

"Stay out of this," Davidson said. "So these men broke into your uncle's room?"

Teddy piped up. "Not successfully, until tonight. The professor had the room booby-trapped."

Hoyt turned to her. "How did you get in without getting bashed?"

"He told us how to disarm it so we could get him his pajamas," Cornelia said. "While we were in the room, Mr. Martino and his friend came through the door."

"Did they assault you?"

"One of them shoved a gun in our faces. The other demanded my uncle's film."

"His what?"

"The professor has a movie camera," Teddy said. "A very nice Eastman. He bought it for himself for Christmas."

"I've seen it," Davidson said. "He was grinding away when I found him in Crystal River."

"He's filmed everything," Cornelia said. "The train, the trees, the river, the alligators. Obviously, he's recorded something these men don't want seen. Something that will reveal who really killed Mr. Janzen."

"Killed? Oh, dear," Hoyt pressed a hand to his face. "A guest arrested for murder. What shall I tell the owners?"

Cornelia punched the door. "He was not arrested for murder! The sheriff had him detained as a witness."

"Witnesses aren't detained," Hoyt said.

"They are if they do something stupid," she grumbled.

The deputy smiled briefly at that line. "At least you know that he's safe tonight. So, these men robbed you at gunpoint?"

"Essentially."

"There were shots," Hoyt said. "Holes in the walls, hole in the doorjamb, blood on the floor."

"Blood?" Davidson looked the ladies and Mitch over. "Who got shot?"

"I winged Mr. Martino," Teddy announced proudly.

Cornelia winced.

"You had a gun?"

"I did. I popped right out of the wardrobe and gave those hoodlums a real surprise."

"You were hiding in the wardrobe?"

"It seemed practical at the time. The men broke in while I was choosing a jacket for the professor."

"And he had a gun in there."

"Not that I know of. It was Cornelia's gun. She always keeps her service revolver in her handbag. So when those thugs had her get the professor's film, I borrowed it."

The deputy shifted back to Cornelia. "You own a gun?"

"Of course; it's for my personal safety. As an army nurse I travel a great deal, sometimes in unsavory places. A woman has to guard her virtue."

Davidson's eyes swept over Cornelia, from her oxford shoes to the gray hair in a granny bun. She straightened to her maximum height, squared her jaw, and glared at him. He sat down on the desk and didn't say anything for a moment. Finally, he pointed at Mitch. "Who's this guy?"

"Our driver," Cornelia stated. "We had him come pick us up in Crystal River. He was helping us carry my uncle's things."

"Uh huh." The deputy took out his notepad and flipped to a fresh page. "And your name?"

"Mitchell Grant."

"Where are you from and what do you do, Mr. Grant?"

"I'm from Tampa, and right now, I'm a driver for the West Coast Development Company."

"You came a long way to be a glorified taxi man."

"I needed the work."

"Needed the work," Davidson said. "Getting lots of tips?"

"I'm doing all right," Mitch said, and gave Teddy a wink.

"So, what do you say happened?"

"I brought the ladies back to town. They asked me to give them a hand, so I did."

110

"You were in the room when these men broke in?"

"Yes."

"What did you do when that happened?"

"I put my hands up. They had guns."

"Oh, don't be modest, Mitch," Teddy said. "You throw even better than Dazzy Vance. That book nailed him right in the eye. And you did a great job chasing them."

Davidson slapped the desk. "For crying out loud! Do you people just want to be killed?"

Cornelia glared at him. "We gave chase because no one else is interested in looking past my uncle for Mr. Janzen's murderer."

"Lady, your uncle is up to his elbows in this or they wouldn't be chasing him. In case you haven't figured it out, those men are hoodlums."

"Well, my uncle is not. Now if you don't mind, I would like to take him his pajamas before the night is over."

The jailer was right about one thing. There was a cozy fire going at the Crystal River City Jail when Cornelia returned. Uncle Percival was still sitting on the edge of his cot, but the night man had pulled a chair over. The old gentleman looked almost as ancient as her uncle, though he lacked the snowy beard and thick white hair. For that matter, he had more hair growing from his ears and broad nose than from the top of his head. The two of them were playing checkers through the bars of the cage.

"About time you folks got back," the night man said. "I was beginning to think you forgot."

"We ran into a couple of thugs who wanted to steal my uncle's film," Cornelia said. "It took us a while to get away from them."

"From what I hear, they were trying to get away from you," the sheriff said, entering the room with the cages.

He closed the door, leaned back against the frame, and rubbed his chin as he considered what to say next.

"Suppose you start at the beginning, and tell me what happened from the time you left here, Miss Pettijohn. Keep in mind that I'm going to be powerful upset with you if I find out later that you left out important details."

His steady gaze did more to unnerve Cornelia than all of his deputy's questions. The sandwich she had eaten in the car weighed like rocks in her stomach. When she started to speak, her mouth was so dry that her voice came out in a rasp.

"We answered Deputy Andy's questions before we left the hotel."

"Andy is a decent deputy, but questions don't always get the whole truth. For instance, he didn't know anything about that little shootout by the river. I want the whole story, Miss Pettijohn, from beginning to end."

Cornelia closed her eyes and let out a long sigh. Judging from the stubborn set of Sheriff Bowden's jaw, an abbreviated version of the night's events wouldn't do. This was going to take a while. It was also likely to land them in the cell beside her uncle, not a prospect she relished.

"I guess it started with me," Mitch said. "I was worried that the ladies were getting caught between the two mobs trying to expand into Citrus County."

Sheriff Bowden's eyes narrowed. "How did you know about that?"

Mitch reached into his pocket with two fingers and took out his press card.

"It was my job to know, Sheriff. Call my editor, if you believe otherwise. I don't know about your men at the *Chronicle*, but I've been following this story since Antinori started moving in on Charlie Wall's operation."

"What interest do Tampa crime lords have in Homosassa?"

"Plenty," Mitch said. "Charlie Wall never was the typical sort of mug that works the angles. He's smart, had a good family, but he turned his back on all that 'cause he saw that a smart man could clean up with his own mob. So he hired some muscle and started up a numbers racket. Now he controls the gambling, prostitution, bootlegging. Anything but dope, not even reefer. He made a deal with the Cubans."

"Get to the point."

"Well, Sheriff, Charlie has lots of dough and no room to expand south, so he's claimed all of central Florida as his turf. He sent a few of his boys up to check out rumors that other mobs were looking for some opportunities north of Tampa. Homosassa's planned casino is a sugarplum just waiting to be nabbed by one of the gangs. Charlie says it's his. Trouble is, Ignacio Antinori's mouth is watering for the same plum."

Mitch leaned against the wall.

"The way I see it, Charlie's got himself a problem. One of his boys and a pile of his money disappeared. Coppers found his bag man sleeping under a pile of fishes but his dough is still missing. He's mad as all get out and determined to learn what happened. His hatchet men are all over the place."

"Where do the ladies and the professor fit into this tale you're spinning?"

"Yes, tell us," Teddy said. "This is so interesting."

Mitch smiled at her before going on. "Aside from sharing a drink and a dance or two with one of Charlie's boys, I think the ladies are only interested in clearing their uncle of any involvement in the Janzen case. At least, that's all they wanted until Antinori's goons took such a keen interest in the professor's movie."

"My movie?" Professor Pettijohn exclaimed. "What do you mean they took a keen interest in my movie?"

"Sorry, Professor. They took your films," Mitch said.

Uncle Percival glared through the bars at Bowden. "Sheriff, that is my private property. Since we know who committed this theft, I expect you to recover it. Cornelia, give him a full report."

Cornelia snarled in frustration. "There's not much he can do now, Uncle Percival. Your film is at the bottom of the river, compliments of Mr. Belluchi and his friend. This evening, they broke into your room and demanded the film at gunpoint. Teddy managed to shoot one of them and Mitch gave the other a shiner, but they got away."

"We gave chase," Teddy chimed in. "It was quite thrilling."

"If by thrilling you mean dangerous and foolhardy," the sheriff said, "then yes, it was. These men are hardened criminals. All of you could have been killed."

Teddy's face flushed. "But they had the film! There might be evidence on that film that would clear the professor. We couldn't let them get away with that."

"Miss Lawless, they did get away with the film. Even if he had filmed someone giving Mr. Janzen a hefty dose of poison, it doesn't do us any good soaking in the mud at the bottom of the river. There is no way of finding out now what, if anything was photographed by Professor Pettijohn. We may have lost valuable evidence."

"Not necessarily," came the barreling voice from the cage.

Every head in the room turned toward the professor. He stood up and stepped to the corner of his tiny cell. His blue eyes twinkled as they traveled from face to face.

Cornelia could tell he was enjoying having everyone's attention riveted on him.

"Out with it, Uncle."

Pettijohn chuckled.

"Eastman packs its motion picture film in metal canisters. I haven't tried submerging one in water, but it is quite possible that those canisters are watertight. If there is a way to recover the film, it could be undamaged by these hooligans' attempts to send it to a watery grave."

"That's all well and good, Professor," the sheriff said, "but how do you propose we retrieve them from the bottom of an alligator-infested river? I'm not going in after it."

"How about one of those Greeks down in Tarpon Springs?" Mitch suggested. "The ones who gather the sponges. They're used to gators and have diving gear."

The sheriff blinked. "Do you have any idea what that would cost? The county isn't going to pay for me to bring in a diver just to get some tourist's movie out of the river."

"I'll pay for it," Professor Pettijohn said, "if you'll let me film the dive."

"Uncle Percival, really? Filming a diver is the least of your worries." Cornelia's face grew hotter with every word.

114

"May I remind you that you are locked up in that cell? You'll pay for the diver and anything he needs to resolve this situation. There are thugs the size of gorillas after us."

"Calm down and stop giving me orders, Corny."

Her eyes bulged. "Calm down? Do I need to remind you that we nearly got killed tonight? What on earth did you film that got us into this much trouble?"

Professor Pettijohn rested his thumb under his jaw and tapped one finger against his temple as he mulled over her last question. "I'm not quite sure."

"Then tell me what's on those films and I'll figure it out."

"Where should I begin?" he asked.

The phone rang and the sheriff rose. "Don't start without me, folks. I want to hear this."

After he left, Cornelia went over to the cell. "With the exception of Rowley, you didn't meet any of these people until Ocala. Start there when the sheriff returns. Don't just tell us what you were filming, tell us every detail of what was going on, even the events that could have been in the background of your film."

Mitch's eyebrows shot up.

"He can do that?"

The professor nodded, then sat down on his cot and closed his eyes.

Sheriff Bowden returned, scowling.

"Has someone else died?' Teddy asked.

"No. Let's start. I'm powerful interested in what your uncle remembers."

They stared at the professor, waiting for him to speak.

The old man's eyes were still closed. "Very well, I'll start with the filming in Ocala. There were some interesting construction methods being employed in building the new courthouse across the street from our hotel. Although that didn't involve any of the people that continued to Homosassa with us."

"Skip ahead then, Uncle. Where did you first film the people that came with us?"

Mitch pulled a notebook and pencil from his pocket.

"If you try to record everything, you're going to need a bigger notebook," Teddy whispered. "Listening to the minutiae of our daily lives in detail would fill the Sunday edition of your paper, not that anyone would want to read it."

"How the blazes can he remember everything?" Mitch whispered back.

"Eidetic memory. It is really quite remarkable—for a little while. After that, it becomes tedious."

Within the first ten minutes of Professor Pettijohn's description of the luncheon the West Coast developers held for prospective investors, Mitch concluded that tedious was a gross understatement. Listening to the professor drone on was worse than when he'd worked the city government beat and had to sit through council meetings. The only useful information was where the suspects were located during lunch. He finished his sketch of the seating arrangement and stood up from his chair to stretch.

Teddy took advantage of the reporter blocking Sheriff Bowden's line of sight and had a generous swig of her medicine. She hoped the scent didn't carry to the other side of the room. There wasn't much danger of anyone else seeing her. Cornelia was engrossed in her uncle's monologue. The night jailer had drifted off and was snoring softly with his head on the checkerboard. Sheriff Bowden was putting up a valiant effort to pay attention, but his chin had dropped toward his chest more than once.

By the time the professor reached the point at the Ocala station where he gave Cornelia the camera, Teddy had completely lost interest in listening. She contented herself with watching the fire through the tiny slots in the front of the stove until her eyelids grew heavy.

"That's it," Cornelia shouted. "Did you hear that, Sheriff?"

She turned and looked at Sheriff Bowden, who had plainly been jolted awake by her outburst.

"Humm...yes. Could you repeat that, Professor?"

"What part do you want me to repeat?"

"Uh..."

Cornelia took mercy on him.

"Start with when the train was finished loading cargo, after most of the fish house crew had departed."

"Right," Sheriff Bowden agreed. "Start there and tell me what happened."

"I'd been filming the train and the bustle of loading. The sun wasn't quite above the horizon, but there was enough light for me to film the bins of fish being loaded to ship north."

"What does this have to do with Janzen's murder?" Mitch asked.

"Nothing," Cornelia snapped. "It was the other fellow. The one they found in Ocala."

Mitch let out a low whistle and started scribbling in his notebook.

"Go on," Sheriff Bowden said.

"I was filming the locomotive on the turntable when a couple of men carrying a heavy load approached the gondolas from the rear. The light back there wasn't good, so I paid no attention to them. Besides, I didn't know them at the time."

"But you know them now?" the sheriff asked.

"Indeed. One of them was the fellow my niece compared to a gorilla. He and his friends are staying at the new hotel."

"Tiny Belluchi?" Mitch asked. "Was his pal Cesare Ricci the other, or was it Leo?"

"Cesare," the professor said. "As I was saying, I was getting a great shot of the engine on the turntable. It seemed like a perfect beginning to my film for the day. The growing light, fish being loaded, the steam coiling round the engine like mist as it rotated..."

"Belluchi, Professor?" the sheriff growled.

"I don't know if he was in my film, or too far to the side. After the brakeman finished inspecting the gondolas, Belluchi and his friend came around the end of the train and dumped the man they were carrying into an empty fish bin. Tiny piled some fish on top of him while his friend got some buckets of ice. Mr. Ricci was facing me when he came back with the ice. He must have seen the camera."

"Professor Pettijohn, why didn't you report this immediately?" the sheriff spluttered. "Even if you didn't see the actual murder, you must have realized you were witnessing a body being disposed of."

"I was filming the train," the professor said defensively. "My focus was there. It is only now, since I have been asked to remember details of the background, that I am aware of what I saw."

"Are you kidding me? You didn't notice that a dead man was being buried in ice about twenty or so feet from your focus?"

"Sheriff, you must understand. When I need to, I can recall the details of everything I see or hear. The images play in my head like a movie. Over the years, I taught myself to concentrate on what I was doing. That is the only way I can block out the plethora of distractions going on in the world. If I were to pay attention to every detail in my field of vision and hearing, I wouldn't get anything done."

"Hell's bells—pardon my language, ladies."

Cornelia stood up, crossed her arms in front of her, and glared at the sheriff.

"The point is, I told you that my uncle didn't have anything to do with the murder. Now will you let him go and lock up the real killers?"

"Miss Pettijohn, what your uncle described may prove to be what happened to that fellow they found in Ocala. It doesn't clear him of Mr. Janzen's murder. In fact, there isn't one bit of evidence connecting the two murders."

Cornelia looked like a boiler on the point of exploding. "Will you at least be releasing him in the morning?"

"That's unlikely, after this evening."

"And why not? You just said that there was no evidence connecting the two crimes."

"There isn't. But, Miss Pettijohn, your uncle's room became a crime scene tonight. It was searched."

"So?"

"A bottle was found in your uncle's valise." He turned back to Percival Pettijohn. "Would you care to explain, sir, why you are in possession of an aspirin bottle containing savin tablets?"

"Okay, so give," Mitch said once they were on the road back to Homosassa. "What's savin?"

"It's a poison from a plant related to juniper. It produces a sour odor when it metabolizes," Teddy said. "No wonder it seemed familiar. I'm surprised neither of us had identified it properly, Cornelia."

Cornelia didn't reply; she was fit to be tied. They had done their own search of the room while gathering clothing for Uncle Percival's night in jail. There was no such bottle in his valise. *She* always carried his medications.

Teddy was busy musing. "But why savin? I can't imagine that he had call for its usual use."

"Which is?" Mitch asked.

"To traumatize a woman's body and produce a miscarriage. It makes a dandy poison for the same reason. You remember my friend in Puerto Rico, Cornelia?"

"Yes," Cornelia mumbled, wishing Teddy would leave her alone. Of course she remembered Puerto Rico and Martha, a nurse stationed there. Martha lost the soldier she loved at San Juan, then discovered that she was pregnant. Rather than face the shame of giving birth out of wedlock, she gambled with one of the patent medicines offered by unscrupulous sellers. Martha purchased one that promised to stop female 'irregularities'. Savin was the main ingredient.

"How would he get hold of something like that?" Mitch asked.

"He didn't," Cornelia retorted. Why wouldn't they both just shut up? "That bottle wasn't in his luggage—we would have seen it when we searched his things. I searched his valise and it wasn't there."

"I can't believe the sheriff thought that *we* might have had that among our own medicines," Teddy said. "We're both well past the age of conceiving."

"He thought we might have been keeping some to aid young girls in trouble," Cornelia snapped. "I informed him that a bad reputation was not lethal, but savin is."

Tears gathered in the corner of Teddy's eyes. "The pain, the vomiting, the odor. Exactly the same symptoms she had. And I didn't even notice."

So that's what was bothering Teddy. Cornelia took her hands and held it between her own. "Don't blame yourself for missing it; no one was going to think savin poisoning with a man. Besides, it has been a long time since Martha died."

The mention of her name brought the whole ugly incident back. Martha had been so young, so full of promise, before her sickness. When her fellow nurses realized how ill their friend was, they all took turns caring for her. Martha confessed the cause of her malady to Teddy, who had trained with her and knew her best. It had been Teddy who attended her death, and Teddy who had convinced the physician to list yellow fever on the death certificate in order to spare Martha's family further pain.

"You're right, dear, but I do feel rather the fool."

"You're not a fool. I'd like to catch the fool, though, who planted that bottle in my uncle's room."

"When do you think it happened?" Mitch asked. "We weren't gone that long, and gunshots tend to discourage visitors. Not to mention the fact that everyone in the hotel knows your uncle booby-traps his room."

"I think we left the door open when we followed the gangsters," Cornelia said. "I'm sure that the true murderer has been keeping track of the police investigation, and word probably traveled fast that my uncle was a suspect. Desperation overcame fear, and he or she seized the opportunity to cement the law's suspicions where Professor Pettijohn was concerned."

"Janzen's killer must have been in the hotel at the time," Teddy said.

"And have access to the evidence," Cornelia added. "Which implies that the murderer was with us on the train, and is also staying at our hotel."

"This trip is getting a little too interesting, even for me," Teddy said.

The corridor to their room was marred by a new feature: a sign declaring the professor's room off-limits. "Keep Out—Order of the Sheriff" was hand-lettered block style on the cardboard.

"At least our luggage isn't waiting for us here in the hall," Cornelia said. She unlocked the door to their room. "Hmm. Things look undisturbed in here."

"We're not as interesting as the professor."

"No one is as interesting as my uncle. Help me check the room for signs of searching or theft."

"Good idea," Teddy said, pulling the drawer to the nightstand open. "Drat. I left my Oreos in the professor's room."

"They should be safe. They're under lock and key, order of the sheriff's department."

"Maybe they have more at the little shop across the street."

"We'll go over when they open."

"You know, Mitch is not the only one who should get some sleep," Teddy said. "No one went to bed last night. Not even your uncle."

Cornelia straightened from her position over her suitcase and sighed. "I'm too angry to sleep right now."

"And worried, perhaps?" Teddy ventured.

"Yes, worried too. I think I'm going to clean up and have breakfast. After breakfast, I'm going to question Mrs. Minyard about her visit to Mr. Janzen's room. The police aren't going to look any further than my uncle, so it's up to me to find the real killer."

Teddy took her arm. "Up to us, dear. Two heads are better than one, they say."

Chapter 11

"Susie seemed surprised at my order," Teddy said as they reentered the hotel, fortified with breakfast. "Is there something wrong with pecan pancakes and a side of ham?"

"Not at all. She just expected your usual order of an ice bag and toast. That's been your daily breakfast since you started attending Chago's parties."

"Nonsense! I've ordered other things."

"Not recently, dear." Cornelia knocked on Helen's door, and Kathleen answered.

"Teddy! Miss Pettijohn. How are you?"

"We're well, thank you. Is your aunt here?"

"Of course. Aunt Helen, the nurses are here. Teddy and her friend."

The woman with salt-and-pepper hair came to the door. Her eyes were eager; news about Uncle Percival must have traveled fast—or was it glee at a successful frame?

"Greetings, ladies. What can I do for you today?"

Cornelia fixed her with a stare. "Mrs. Minyard. You and I need to talk. Perhaps Teddy could take your niece sightseeing for a bit."

"But I want to stay!" Teddy protested. "I could help grill her."

Panic flickered in Helen Minyard's eyes.

"No, Teddy, I would prefer to speak to her privately. Besides, Kathleen shouldn't be wandering around alone. There are predators here. Mrs. Minyard—?"

"Yes," Helen sighed. "Please go with her, dear. This may be tiresome for you."

Teddy's expression was sullen as she left with Kathleen.

Cornelia was relieved that she relented, though she knew from their long history together that she was going to pay for excluding Teddy later.

Once the pair was out of earshot, Cornelia closed the door and sat in one of the chairs.

Helen paced the floor. "I have an idea of what has happened recently, Miss Pettijohn. Please accept my condolences and my wish that your uncle is soon free of trouble."

"My thanks. Those are also my wishes, and one of the reasons I'm calling on you so early. Recently, I was on the second floor of the Homosassa Hotel looking for a person... a person I needed information from. While I was there, I saw you coming out of Raymond Janzen's room."

"Really, Miss Pettijohn!" Mrs. Minyard clutched her long strand of beads. "I understand your concern, but casting suspicion on others will do you no good. We have been cleared to leave by Sheriff Bowden, and we will be departing on the train Monday."

"It's more than merely casting suspicion," Cornelia pressed. "I know it was you, and I know very well which room you were visiting, since I was there when the man died. If I were to tell Sheriff Bowden what I saw, I'm sure he would at least look into it. If he does, will he find no connection between you?"

Helen seemed to deflate as she sank into the other chair. "I didn't kill him."

"I never said that you did."

"But you would find it very helpful if I had, wouldn't you? I went to his room because—" she looked out her window for witnesses, "—because he had something very dear to me. I wanted it back."

"What was it?"

She entreated Cornelia with her eyes. "You were in the War. You know how many young men were lost."

Cornelia's voice softened. "Yes, I know. Too many good boys."

"My son was one of them. Albert Junior. He didn't even fall in battle. He died in an infirmary of the Spanish Flu."

"That is doubly tragic." To travel and risk so much, to die of something he could have died from at home. "My own father passed away from the Spanish Influenza."

"Then you understand our grief. After we received the cable about his death, Raymond Janzen came to call. He brought a letter from our son—the last letter he wrote, when he was in the hospital and realized that he was dying. Such a bittersweet gift."

"Yes," the old nurse whispered, remembering how many such letters she had delivered to grieving families from so many wars, too many. San Juan, the Philippines, Mexico, France... when would it end?

"That letter was the last thing we received from our son. But there was Raymond, his good friend. He took an apartment in Wilmington near ours, visited us. I asked him one day, 'Shouldn't you be with your own family?' and he told me that he had none left."

Unpleasant thoughts began forming in Cornelia's mind. "So he adopted you as his parents."

"Yes, and we saw him as a connection to the son we lost." Her face was dark with remembered pain.

"It didn't end well." Cornelia stated. She'd heard this sort of story before.

"Al—Albert Senior, my husband—hired him to work in our furniture store. His Army experience as a quartermaster served him well, and he was quickly promoted from floor manager to general manager. He oversaw the books."

"He stole from you."

Silent tears slid down her face. "Two sets of accounts. Raymond fooled us for over a year. He embezzled enough to ruin the business, and drained the separate account we used for taxes."

"Horrible." There were no other words she could think of. Cornelia reached out and clasped Helen's hand.

"I haven't told you the worst part," Helen continued. "My husband was ruined, and the government wanted their due. I offered Albert what little money I had from my inheritance, but he refused. He said my funds wouldn't cover the taxes, and he wanted me to be left with something. I found out later what he meant. While I was visiting the parson, he took out his father's gun and... ended his life."

Cornelia nodded. "So you came here to find Raymond Janzen again."

"One of my friends received a publicity flyer for the Homosassa project. She recognized his picture and gave it to me." Mrs. Minyard's upper lip curled with the words.

"And you brought your niece to help you kill him?"

"No! Dear Lord, no. I brought Kathleen with me because she can't stand her mother and I was afraid to travel alone. I would never ask her to participate in a crime."

"You followed him here. You broke into his room. Was it his money you wanted, then? As repayment?"

"No. I wanted something far more dear to me." Helen reached into her purse, brought out a folded handkerchief. She unwrapped the cotton cloth and showed Cornelia its contents.

"Albert's watch. It was a gift from his father. He intended to leave it to our son, but Albert Junior died. He gave it to Raymond instead. Before we knew who and what he really was."

Cornelia took the watch, studied it. The engraved inscription read: "Albert Minyard, 1860. *Eruditio et Religio*". It must have been as precious to him as her nurse's pin was to her. She remembered the trip on the Express then, the conversations she'd overheard.

"You said you would get this back if you had to pry it from his cold dead fingers. When we were getting on board the train."

"Yes. That was more a figure of speech than anything else. I intended to confront him, preferably in a public place for safety, and demand the watch back. At first, I thought the binder boy's claims of his illness were lies. I concluded he had seen me and wished to avoid the consequences of his actions. But then he died, and I only had one chance to get the watch back before it disappeared along with his belongings to the police, or was sold to help pay for his burial."

"How did you get into the room?"

Helen bit her lower lip, the way a young girl would. "I waited for the maid to open the door, then approached her

126

with a request to take a pair of sunglasses to my niece. That, and a nice tip."

Meanwhile, Teddy and Kathleen had decided not to sightsee. The young woman really didn't know how to apply lipstick yet, so Teddy decided to give her lessons.

"Now for the upper lip. You want to exaggerate the line a little to make that Cupid's Bow."

"My lip doesn't go up that pointy."

Teddy laughed. "I don't think most people's lips do. That's part of the illusion. Wait—" She reached into her makeup bag. "I've got a cheat for you."

Kathleen stared at the rectangle of metal. "Is that a lip stencil? I wanted to get one, but Mother wouldn't hear of it."

"Take it, then. What Mother doesn't know won't hurt you."

Kathleen giggled.

After more fun with cosmetics, the girl became serious. "I don't mean to be rude, but what did happen to your lungs?"

Teddy thought before answering. "I was gassed near Verdun during the Grand Offensive. Really, I was very fortunate; it was only chlorine gas."

"How could chlorine gas be fortunate?"

"The mustard gas was far worse. I could have been blinded, too, or burned all over my skin."

Kathleen's brow puckered. "Didn't... didn't they keep the nurses away from the really dangerous places?"

"They tried. Sometimes danger was unavoidable if you wanted to help the wounded. Cornelia and I overstepped our bounds a few times."

One too many times. The memories returned, unbidden and undeniable. The faces of the desperate men at Verdun.

"I can't imagine your friend overstepping bounds," Kathleen said. She selected a shade of blush and began brushing it onto her cheek. "She seems so... proper."

"She's principled," Teddy managed. "Not quite the same thing." She tried to focus on the present, but failed.

The Germans pressed the Allies on all sides, and the nurses were forbidden to venture out. The risk of losing even more lives was too great.

Cornelia wouldn't stand for abandoning the wounded. With Teddy's help at lock picking, they liberated the ambulance of a dead corpsman and headed for the front. Explosions and fire echoed around them as they crested the hills, leaving the road when the holes outpaced the pavement. They bore down on the trench of doughboys—boys they knew personally—and clambered over the dirt to reach the injured.

One of the men had to be carried out by litter. Cornelia and the field medic were loading the patient into the vehicle when the gongs sounded, warning of a gas attack. A yellowish cloud filled the sky and descended on them. Teddy closed her eyes and kept holding the pressure bandage tight over the sergeant's femoral artery. He wore her mask. Her throat, her lungs burned. A soldier draped a wet cloth over her head for protection once she was in the open-air vehicle, but she felt like a nun riding a sleigh into hell.

"Are you all right?" Kathleen was shaking her shoulder. "Please say something."

Teddy came back to the present, to safety and clear air, and realized that she'd frightened the child. "I'm sorry, dear. Talking about it makes me remember. I try not to."

"I didn't mean to do that," the girl said. "I guess I was too nosy. I apologize."

"No need to apologize," she replied. "It was a natural question."

Once Teddy returned, Cornelia shared what she had learned from Helen Minyard.

"What did you decide to do, after she told you those things?" Teddy asked.

"I gave her the watch back. I have no reason to disbelieve her at this time, and the watch does seem to support her story."

"No chance she could have poisoned Mr. Janzen?"

"If you had defrauded a woman's husband and absconded with a family heirloom, would you willingly eat or drink anything she provided?"

"Not knowingly. But what if she slipped the poison into his food or drink?"

"When would she have had the opportunity? They were staying at different hotels, eating in different places, and he showed symptoms before he left the train."

"What about before he got on the train?"

The thought hadn't occurred to Cornelia. "The part about 'cold dead fingers' would take on new meaning in that context. In that case, though, she had no reason to keep pestering his binder boy the following day. Once would have been enough to tell her whether the poison had worked or not."

Teddy tapped her cane on the floor. "I still can't believe I didn't know it was savin."

"Don't torment yourself, dear. I'm inclined to believe Mrs. Minyard's story. If she'd planned the crime, she would have fabricated a better excuse for breaking into the room."

"Ignorance provides the alibi."

"Ignorance is our problem. We don't know enough about Mr. Janzen."

"He was definitely a bounder, as Mr. Hofstetter put it."

"Yes, but to a larger group of people than we originally thought. I doubt Mr. Vance could throw a baseball in Homosassa without hitting someone with a grudge against Mr. Janzen. Not that I want to test that theory. Janzen may have cheated baseball players, too."

"Whom do we grill next, if Mrs. Minyard is innocent?"

Cornelia thought for a moment. "Peter Rowley, I should think. He was Deputy Davidson's original prime suspect and, from the conversation we couldn't help but overhear, had a reason to wish the man dead."

"Should we find him now?"

"I don't think we have time," Cornelia said, checking the watch pinned to her chest. "The sheriff was going to call the sponge company as soon as it opened. We need to find out whether they're coming or not."

Teddy was busy admiring the dive crew. For that matter, so was everyone else in Homosassa. Tourists and locals alike crowded the riverbank, vying for a spot with a better view of the muscular young men. A few of the women twittered about how handsome and exotic the Greek fishermen were with their thick black hair and large dark eyes.

Each man knew his job without any direction. Two young Greek men tested the compressor, said something Cornelia could not understand, and made some adjustments. The others unloaded the heavy diving equipment and spread it out on the grass. One yelled "Alexandros" followed by a string of words Cornelia presumed were Greek.

The diver nodded and came over. Together, the three-man team dressed him in his airtight suit, checking and rechecking every article. Then they reeled out a long rope and laced it through the collar of his suit, between his legs, back up the other side of his suit, and repeated the process on the back. To Cornelia, the way the ropes were configured resembled the harness of a plow mule.

Once the suit was in place, the diver walked to the water's edge and sat down. He took off his shoes and said something to the crew that made them all laugh as they put the heavy dive boots on him and laced them tight. Then they brought the helmet over, put it on him, and bolted it in place.

"Alexandros," Teddy said, "just like in the *Iliad*, but in different armor."

Deputy Davidson stayed close to his prisoner, his chest puffed out, and his hand on the hilt of his revolver. Not that the posturing did him any good. The visitors and the locals were all watching the dive crew. Those with cameras posed for pictures as close to the diver as they dared.

Cornelia saw that it was the equipment that held the professor's attention. The portable compressor in its fine-grained wooden case, the polished brass fittings attaching the gauges were too attractive for him to resist. He marveled audibly over the great rubber suit with iron-weighted rubber boots and a helmet of iron and brass. To a man as fascinated by mechanical devices as the professor, filming the helmet being bolted onto the diver was not to be missed. He caught every moment of the airline being attached, the men helping Alexandros to his feet, and the strange suit inflating.

Deputy Davidson was oblivious to the history being made. He kept eyeing the elderly man as if he were a bank robber hoping to stage an escape on the diver's back.

Cornelia wasn't sure which was worse: the mob of onlookers Sheriff Bowden was trying to control, or her uncle positioning himself perilously close to the air compressor flywheel to get a better angle for his camera.

She overheard one of the deputies saying that the fishermen had come early to feed the alligators so they wouldn't bother the diver, but gawking locals in their johnboats were another matter. The water was so thick with them, she didn't see how the diver would be able to keep his line from being fouled.

Sheriff Bowden must have had the same fears. He shouted through a megaphone to be heard above the din of noise, but eventually he managed to get the boatmen to clear the area where Alexandros needed to dive. Once that was done, the diver picked up his equipment and walked slowly into the water until he disappeared under the surface, leaving only a trail of air bubbles to mark his progress.

On the riverbank, the crowd grew quiet. The minutes ticked by. Sweat trickled down the back of Cornelia's neck. She watched the river, barely breathing, as though taking in too much air would deprive the man walking below the water of his share. Around her, the crush of bodies became oppressive. She was annoyed by buzzing insects. The scent of stale sweat, fish, even the usual damp earthy smell of the river made her stomach churn. Her hands clenched and unclenched as she waited, worried that the film would not be found, or that the film canisters were not as watertight as her uncle believed.

There was a tug on the rope tether, and a crewman fed out another twenty feet of rope.

Cornelia stood on tiptoe to see over the head of a pushy farmer who trampled her feet until she was forced to make room for him. On the riverbank, she could see one of the men pulling the rope out of the water. There was a cheer from the crowd as the diver's net bag was pulled ashore and Uncle Percival's ruined film case was opened.

The sheriff and a couple of his men came over to claim the bag. After that, it was impossible for Cornelia to see anything but the backside of police uniforms until she spotted Deputy Davidson making his way through the crowd, carrying the film. A moment later he got in his car, cranked the siren to clear a path, and sped away from the river.

"They took all my film," the professor grumbled. "Sheriff Bowden wouldn't even let me have the unopened ones still in the box."

"You should be happy the sheriff let you out of jail long enough to see this," Cornelia said. "After all the trouble you've caused, it would have been more logical to keep you there."

"But I used the last of the reel in my camera filming the dive. There is no place to buy more. We'll probably have to go all the way to Saint Petersburg or Tampa to find a camera shop that carries moving picture film."

"Good, you can put that fool camera away and help us figure out who's trying to frame you for murder."

"Are you sure they're trying to frame me, Corny?"

"Don't call me Corny. And yes, I'm sure. That bottle of savin didn't get in your room by accident. Someone put it there after I searched the room."

His brilliant blue eyes widened. "Why were you searching my room?"

"Because you keep lying to me." She tried to look severe. It was all an act. No matter how much trouble he gave her, Cornelia adored the old man. It was impossible to stay mad at him for more than a few minutes. She wasn't about to let him know that, though.

"I haven't lied to you. I simply neglected to tell you every detail of my plans."

"When I broke your friend Doc Haydon's microscope slides, you told me that lies of omission were as dishonest as the ones we tell."

The professor's cheeks turned a rose color that made him look even more like Santa. "The crowd is dispersing. Shall

132

we find your friend Mitch to take you back to the hotel?" he said. "I'm sure you girls are exhausted."

Andy Davidson cruised along with the windows down, ignoring the cloud of dust billowing behind his black and tan. He loved the sound of shells crushing under the tires. Every fall the county graded the road and put down another three or four inches of shells. They were cheaper and more plentiful than gravel. Besides, it didn't matter what you put on the roads; when the rainy season hit, the sandy ground sucked paving materials into the depths and the ruts returned.

He was glad that the weather was warm enough for open air driving. The mud-soaked bag in the passenger floorboard stank of fish and river muck. Other than that, getting the goofy professor's film developed was a great excuse to see if his new sheriff's department car lived up to the advertisements. Once he hit the paved section of Tampa Road, he was going to open her up and see if he really could do forty miles-per-hour. *Wouldn't that be something?*

The part of the Dixie Highway that ran through Citrus County was a fancy-named dirt road. Paved highways were further south. Word was that between Oldsmar and Tampa there was a divided highway with asphalt so smooth that you could drive for miles without hitting a single bump. He'd never seen a road like that.

It took him more than an hour to reach Tarpon Springs, thanks to a tractor he followed for at least five miles before the road widened enough him to pass. Half an hour later, he noticed a black Ford in the rear view mirror. Andy couldn't see the driver, but something about the vehicle made him nervous.

He tried speeding up, then slowing down. Either way, the Ford stayed about the same distance behind him. It was still there when he rounded a curve a too fast and nearly smacked into the disabled Packard blocking the road.

Andy stood on the brakes.

That's when he noticed the barrel of a shotgun coming out from under the hood of the Packard.

He threw his car into reverse. The gears ground as he lurched backwards.

The Ford was coming up behind him fast. Too fast.

Shells flew out from under his car as he stepped on the accelerator. He had to cut sharply to the left to avoid a large live oak.

There was no avoiding the bushels of Spanish moss hanging from the branches, though, as he drove through someone's lawn. Each soft thud deposited another pile onto his windshield, making it harder to see the road ahead.

The sheriff was going to have his hide for the damage he was doing to the county's new car, but Andy wasn't about to let the driver overtake him.

A shotgun blast took out the rear side window when he passed the Packard.

The Ford was still with him.

His accelerator was on the floor. He still pressed harder.

Through a cloud of dust, he could see he was pulling away from the Ford, but the Packard joined the chase and was gaining ground fast.

There was another blast from the shotgun, taking out his right rear tire. Deputy Andy careened out of control. In an instant, the rapid thumping of the flat stopped with a loud snap. Out of the corner of his eye, he saw his rear wheel bounce past him. It bounced a couple more times before rolling into a ditch. Meanwhile, the back end of the car spread a stream of sparks as it scraped the shells from the road and crushed them into dust under its steel frame. The sound sickened him.

Seconds dragged by as he fought to recover from the skid.

The steering wheel was real and solid. Andy clutched it as though he were drowning and the smooth leather was his only lifeline. His hands ached from the effort of holding on...to the wheel...to his nerve...to life.

When it was over, he closed his eyes and took a couple deep breaths, thankful that he was still alive.

His respite was short lived. Andy's stomach knotted at the sound of a pump action shotgun expelling the spent shell that caused his skid. Andy glanced at the Colt holstered in the seat beside him. It might as well have been back at his house. There was no way he could get to his pistol before the shotgun took his head off.

"Don't even think about it, son," the hoodlum said.

Andy wasn't capable of thought with a shotgun barrel inches from his head, though it would have been imprudent to say that.

"Keep those hands right where they are, and nobody has to get hurt."

"Willy, get the bag." the man, perhaps six foot two, ordered. "Then get moving. The boss don't like waiting."

A thin young man with oily hair opened the passenger door and took the professor's film bag. Then he lifted Andy's pistol. "I'd better take this too," he said, "just so you don't get any ideas."

"Give me the handcuffs."

The third man man loosened them from the belt and handed the cuffs to his partner. "Just put them on him and get out of here."

Andy winced as the cuffs clicked tight around his wrist.

His oily captor grinned at him. "I always wanted to do this." He laced the other cuff through the steering wheel and locked it around Andy's left wrist.

"No hard feelings," the big man said when the Ford passed them. "The boss just wants a première of the old guy's moving picture show. When I get to town I'll send you a tow truck."

Chapter 12

The ladies were finishing an early dinner when a familiar figure appeared on the patio.

"Ladies," Sheriff Bowden said. "I hate to disturb your meal, but I have some unfortunate news."

"Uncle Percival. Something's happened?" Cornelia began to rise, but the sheriff waved her back down.

"Your uncle's fine, ma'am. No, something else has happened. Mind if I sit?"

"By all means."

"Thank you," Bowden said. "It's been a long day, and it just got longer. The Tampa police contacted me. Seems they got an anonymous call that Deputy Davidson's car had an accident. They found the car on the side of the road, with one wheel missing."

"And the deputy?"

"They found him in the driver's seat, locked in his own handcuffs. His pride is wounded, but that's all. Being alive means a lot, considering that the description he gave of the men pursuing him sounded like a couple of Charlie Wall's boys. They took the film."

"Oh, no," Teddy said.

"Seems everybody wants to get their hands on this film of your uncle's."

"What will you do now?" Cornelia asked.

"Go ahead with the investigation, but the film would have helped a lot. Your uncle just became a whole lot more important, too. I don't know how a jury is going to feel about his weird memory, or the fact he can't hear thunder without that pocket contraption he uses, but he's the only witness we have."

"Does that mean you are going to let him out of jail?" Cornelia asked.

The sheriff frowned. His fingers drummed on the table as he considered the question. "I think he is better off where he is, for now. No offense, Miss Pettijohn. Your uncle is a little too headstrong for his own good. They've called an arraignment for tomorrow."

He saw the anger flash in her eyes and held up his hand. "I've spoken to Judge Bullock on his behalf. Honest, ma'am, the prosecutor is not going to charge him with Mr. Janzen's murder without more information. He's just asking the judge to keep your uncle from traipsing off before we figure out the truth."

Before Cornelia could come up with a plausible defense of her uncle's behavior, Sheriff Bowden stood up. "As much as I enjoy charming company, there is work to be done. I'll let you ladies get back to your dinner."

"Humph," Cornelia grunted when he was out of earshot. "At the rate he is losing evidence, Sheriff Bowden is never going to find who killed Mr. Janzen. That man will keep Uncle Percival in that tiny cage until he catches something dreadful. I guess it is up to us to clear his good name."

"Are we going to grill more suspects?" Teddy asked.

Cornelia lowered her head into the palm of her hand and groaned. "Where do you get these notions?" Her voice sounded gruff, but a trace of a smile gave the game away. Teddy's impetuous nature always amused her, no matter how much Cornelia felt like an old grizzly bear.

"Where do we start?" Teddy asked when her companion stopped growling.

"I saw Mr. Rowley duck out when he spotted the sheriff. He must be around somewhere. Why don't you tell the kitchen that we would like a pot of tea in the lounge? Meanwhile, I'll locate our missing salesman."

Rowley and Cornelia entered the lounge and sat down across from Teddy.

"Tea?" Teddy indicated the tray. "I just ordered a fresh pot."

"On a cold evening like this?" Rowley said. "Great."

"If you think it's cold today, it must get quite warm in the summer." Teddy filled a cup for him. "Sugar?"

"One lump. The summers definitely get warm here. Not as bad as Miami, but pretty hot."

They all sipped their tea. Teddy glanced at Cornelia, Cornelia glanced at her. Rowley watched them both, and then spoke.

"I thank you for the invitation, ladies. I—er—notice that the Professor isn't here. Have you decided to purchase your own home?"

"No," Cornelia said, "we invited you here to discuss a person. Raymond Janzen."

Rowley's face darkened and he clenched his jaw, deepening the cleft in his chin. "I'd prefer not to. The man is dead and I have nothing good to say about him. From what's happened with your uncle, you know what sort of man he was."

"Neither Cornelia nor I had heard of him before this trip," Teddy said. "But his death seems to have landed us in the soup right beside you."

"You've been talking to Deputy Davidson, I see."

"No, dear," Teddy patted his knee, "but we couldn't help noticing that you were his prime suspect."

"Yeah, well, there's something you don't know. When I went to serve in the Great War, I left my best friend and my fiancée behind. When I returned, I didn't have either one."

Teddy formed a moue with her lips. "I presume the friend was Andy?"

"You presume correctly. Alice was my fiancée. I wrote her all the time during the War, and she wrote me. I thought everything was fine till I got a letter from her one week before I was due to be shipped home. She'd married him. The year before. And she didn't tell me."

Another sad outcome of the war, Cornelia thought. She'd had to deliver letters like that to many wounded soldiers, and in a few cases even read them aloud for a patient, which meant she and his wardmates were also privy to his humiliation.

"How rotten of her!" Teddy squeezed his forearm. "Any girl who had a handsome and honorable man like you should have counted herself lucky."

"Uh, thanks, ma'am. If you'd just meant to offer me your sympathy, I'm grateful. But I don't know anything else, and there are clients I need to—" He half-rose.

"Sit down, Sergeant Rowley," Cornelia said in a tone that brooked no disobedience. He complied immediately. "I apologize for your discomfort, but it is necessary in this case. Since the time we attended Lieutenant Janzen in his final illness, we have dealt with break-in attempts at our hotel."

He nodded. "I know, ma'am. I apologize. Are you saying that you think they're connected?"

Cornelia nodded. It was stretching things a wee bit, but at least one break-in had been to plant evidence. "In the last day or so, several unsavory acts on Janzen's part have come to our attention. I understand that you, or rather your brother, might have been one of his victims. For reasons you are undoubtedly familiar with, we are now strongly motivated to learn more about him and the life he led."

"I can see why, but I didn't poison him. And I promise you, I didn't try to break in on your uncle. No dirt in my hair."

"Oh, we don't think you did it," Teddy said. "We have other sus-ow!" She shifted in her chair, moving her ankles out of Cornelia's reach.

"What we need is information," Cornelia said, keeping her eyes on Peter. "Please tell us what happened to your brother. You will receive a less biased hearing from us than the deputy has given you."

Rowley rubbed his forehead, and then clasped his hands. "Janzen worked as the quartermaster for our unit during the War. Everything was fine at first, but then we fell low on supplies. He'd tell us he'd ordered more, but we were always short."

"You suspected that something else was going on."

"Not at first. I mean, everyone was making sacrifices. He told us that supplies had been diverted to this or that place along the front. Lots of shooting going on, so who were we to suspect him of lying? Who were we supposed to complain to?"

Cornelia's dour expression became more so. "The shortages continued."

"Yeah." He looked down at his hands. "It all came to a head in the summer before the war ended. We were strung out in the trenches and we—we ran out of ammo. The Krauts swarmed and slaughtered us."

"One of them was your brother."

"Stevie." His voice softened. "My big brother. He sent me to one of the rear positions when he realized that our supplies were coming to an end. I lived. He didn't."

Poor lad. Guilty because his brother had chosen Peter's life over his, and then dumped by his fiancée. "You must have been very angry."

"Not as much as I was later. Jennings Bowden—that's the sheriff's son—worked as a quartermaster for one of the other companies. When we met after the Armistice, he told me there were rumors that Janzen was selling our supplies to the Germans and pocketing the cash. No one could prove anything, though."

"And you wrote Alice about it," Teddy said. "You had to tell someone."

Rowley snorted a half-laugh, but there was no humor in it. "I wrote her, and she reminded Andy about it the other day. Made me a prime suspect."

Cornelia wished Janzen were still alive, so she could strangle him herself. The betrayal of those boys... "Tell me more about the man himself," she managed to say in even tones. "Where he was from, how he came to be in the Army."

"He was Floridian, actually. From St. Augustine, not this area."

"Was his family military? A man like the one you describe would hardly volunteer." There were less dangerous places to cheat people, as proven by Mrs. Minyard's story.

"His dad was a minister. Janzen couldn't get away from him fast enough, went to college up north as soon as he was old enough. Virginia, I think. He said something about it when

I got dumped. Said I was better off, that he'd had to leave Virginia because of girl trouble."

"A college student might be made a quartermaster, yes. I can't picture him earning a field commission."

"No, I can't either."

"You didn't confront him on the train?"

Rowley shrugged. "I know that sounds like I'm lying, but I don't think I even spotted him. He might have seen me, though, and decided to duck me. I met Malcolm Hofstetter when the conductor brought him to my car. He said that Hofstetter had been in a fight and I should keep an eye on him. So, I did."

That cleared Rowley for the time immediately after the fight, but not before. If he were lying about seeing Janzen, though, he might have tried poison. The only problem was the same one they had encountered with Mrs. Minyard: Janzen wouldn't have been foolish enough to eat or drink anything Rowley gave him.

"Thank you for coming here, and for telling us about your brother, Mr. Rowley. You've given us plenty to think about. I know it was difficult for you."

He stood. "That's okay, ladies. You just stay safe. The sheriff's a good man. He will find out who killed Janzen."

Cornelia's fists were clenched so tight that blood couldn't circulate. Her voice dropped an octave and took on the cold tone that had earned her the nickname "The Iron Petticoat."

"I have little evidence that Sheriff Bowden is a good man. He thinks my uncle killed Janzen. He is holding him in a tiny cage because the real killer planted evidence in his room."

The steel in her blue eyes made Rowley trip on the wingback he'd vacated in an attempt to escape. He righted himself before he fell, and mumbled an apology as he fled the lounge.

Once he was gone, Teddy sighed and took off her spectacles. "That wasn't very promising. We're finding plenty of people with reason to want him dead, but no one seems to have done it."

"We know a little more about his background, which is helpful," Cornelia said. "The part about girl trouble was interesting."

"Mrs. Minyard is too old for him, although it would make her a much more interesting person. Kathleen would have still been in pigtails when he was in college. The Carsons are from Virginia."

"Yes, but Rosemary is also older than him and already married."

Teddy half-smiled. "So?"

"You have such a naughty mind. It's one of the things I love about you," Cornelia said. "If Rosemary was the 'girl' he had trouble with, we still have the same problem we have with the others: why would he eat or drink anything she offered him?"

"But we know he did eat or drink something. The savin was ingested."

"We need someone who was near him on the train. Someone besides Uncle Percival. Someone who might have unknowingly witnessed the poisoning."

Teddy shrugged. "We've questioned every potential witness here. The Carsons rode in the other railcar. We'll need to go to the new hotel. Perhaps Mr. Hofstetter is still there. He rode in the other car, too, but he spotted Janzen before then. He could have seen something."

"No luck there. The sheriff released him."

"Drat. Well, there's the man's binder boy."

"Yes," Cornelia replied. "Let's give our favorite driver a call in the morning."

Mitch was outside and ready to escort the ladies to the new hotel long before Teddy found a hat she thought serious enough to wear while she questioned potential murderers.

Cornelia's attempts to help with the selection were useless. Her companion didn't value her opinion when making fashion choices. After a quarter of an hour, she gave up and joined Mitch beside the sedan.

"I thought Miss Theodora was accompanying you," he said.

"She'll be down shortly."

Mitch waited for further explanation, but none was forthcoming. "Whom are you planning to question at the hotel?" he asked after a minute or so.

Cornelia ignored his question.

"Look," Mitch said, "I've leveled with you. Now you need to level with me."

Teddy picked that moment to stroll out of the hotel in an ensemble that stopped conversation. Her "serious" hat turned out to be a pale gray fedora that belonged to the professor. Teddy paired it with a smart blue silk suit and grey oxfords. Cornelia noticed that Teddy had also appropriated her white silk scarf to use as a cravat, no doubt to hide the ruffles on her blouse.

"How did you get that hat?" Cornelia asked, when Teddy joined them. "Uncle Percival's room is a crime scene."

"It was at the front desk. The manager gave it to me yesterday. I'm sure the professor won't mind."

Mitch coughed to cover a chuckle.

Cornelia's shoulders squared. Her glare sucked all humor from the moment.

"You look marvelous, Miss Theodora," he said. "I'm sure suspects will be unable to resist telling you their darkest secrets."

"What dark secrets are *you* hiding?" Cornelia asked.

"None; it leaves my mind open for other peoples'," Mitch replied. "Where are we headed?"

"Nowhere, it seems." Teddy said, as the sheriff's car pulled in beside them.

"Sorry to delay you ladies," Sheriff Bowden said, as he climbed out of his car, "but I need to ask you about some things."

Cornelia waited.

"When you entered the sickroom, what state was it in? Neat, messy?"

"Overall, the room was neat," Cornelia said. "The bed and area surrounding it were less so. Illness, especially nausea, tends to supersede tidiness."

"Mm-hmm." He made a note. "Where were his suitcase, his clothing, and so forth?"

She had to stop to think about that. "His property wasn't uppermost on my mind. His suitcase was in the closet, some coats were hanging there. Oh, and he had a bag of toiletries in the bathroom. Razor, mustache brush, and the like."

"Very good. I'd hate to see what you would remember if it had been uppermost in your mind. Do you recall another bag? A briefcase, perhaps?"

Teddy spoke up. "I do. It was next to the suitcase in the closet. I saw it when I was looking for clean sheets. There were none there, and I had to go to the front desk for more."

Bowden updated his notes. "You can confirm that the briefcase was there?"

"Indeed, quite handsome, too. It was made of red leather and the straps had gold buckles."

"You have an eye for pretty things."

"Yes, she does," Cornelia said. "Since you asked specifically about the briefcase, I presume something has happened to it?"

"We released the room this morning, and Deputy Davidson collected Mr. Janzen's personal property," Bowden said. "The register says he had three bags, but only two were present in the room."

"And his binder boy told you that the briefcase was missing?" She tried to remember if Helen Minyard had been carrying anything when she left the room. No, the only thing Cornelia saw in her mental picture was a shoulder bag. That wouldn't have been large enough to hide a briefcase.

"I was unable to interview the binder boy. Mr. Janzen was supposed to be a land speculator, though, and I've never seen a land speculator that didn't carry his paperwork with him. So, I figured it was a briefcase."

"How clever," Teddy said.

"You weren't able to interview the lad?" Cornelia remembered the blond boy, the one who had rushed into the crowded great hall of the Homosassa Hotel. "His command of

English wasn't very good, but I speak some German. Perhaps I could help translate for you."

"Language isn't the problem. The binder boy's name was Dani Hegstad?"

Cornelia nodded.

"He's gone missing."

"Missing?" Her face reflected the disbelief in her voice. "He was so helpful and concerned when he came looking for a doctor to help Mr. Janzen. Why would such a responsible young man go anywhere? You made it perfectly clear that nobody was allowed to leave."

Sheriff Bowden leaned back against the door of his car and took off his hat. His gaze met Cornelia's. "That didn't stop your uncle from traipsing off, did it?"

"So you think he's on the lam?" Teddy said.

"Theodora! Where do you pick up such language?"

"Don't be an old fuddy-duddy, Corny. It's the twentieth century."

Now he's got her calling me that.

The sheriff cleared his throat. "Don't worry ladies; I've got two deputies out looking for him, and we've contacted Ocala and Jacksonville. He won't get far. Now, if you will excuse me, I've got to get back to work."

Cornelia turned her attention to Mitch. "I am sorry to have wasted your time. It appears we won't be needing a driver after all."

"I do," Teddy said. "If we aren't going to grill that binder boy, it's time to do some shopping."

"Please, not more clothing. There's no room in the car."

"Kathleen and her aunt were discussing a new golfing outfit last night. I'm not a golfer, but you and your uncle play. We'll just have a look around for a belated birthday present. Our gift was going to be a swell party, but the sheriff squashed that. Besides, if we bump into Mrs. Minyard, you could ask her advice about what to buy."

"What are you going to do while I'm talking to Mrs. Minyard?"

"Question her niece. And, afterwards, we're going to put the hotel on standby for Monday. If your uncle gets sprung, we're going to have that birthday party."

Teddy spotted Kathleen the instant they walked through the door of the hotel's pro shop. The young blonde was standing outside the ladies' dressing room looking bored. As they approached, Kathleen's aunt stepped out of the dressing room wearing a smart sports ensemble that made Teddy think she should take up golf just to show off her legs in those knee socks and short pants.

"I'm not sure this is appropriate for someone my age," she heard Mrs. Minyard say as they approached.

"Nonsense, Aunt Helen." Kathleen replied. "The square neck and long waist suit you. You look smashing."

"Smashing is not the look I intended. I need to find something a little less..."

"Revealing," Cornelia replied.

"Exactly," Helen said, retreating to the dressing room.

Teddy opened her purse and lifted her flask enough for Kathleen to see. "I was thinking of going to the clubhouse for lemonade while Cornelia looks for a birthday present for her uncle. Would you like to join me?"

"Aunt Helen wants me to help her find a new golfing outfit."

"It appears that your aunt doesn't agree with your taste any more than Cornelia does mine."

"You have excellent taste, Teddy dear, but smashing isn't my look either." Cornelia turned to Kathleen. "If you will keep Theodora out of trouble, I would be happy to help your aunt find a golfing outfit more to her liking."

The clubhouse provided some welcome coolness from the morning sun. Teddy and Kathleen ordered lemonade before choosing comfortable seats. When the tall glasses arrived, they both sipped the cool liquid. Then, Teddy took the flask out and added a liberal dose of Mr. Scroggins' best to both drinks. Kathleen stirred it, took a sip, and licked her lips.

"That's a little warm going down."

"The ice helps. On the bright side, it makes it a little sweeter."

Their conversation started with fashion; Kathleen complimented Teddy on her choice of hats, and Teddy asked her opinion on henna combs. The girl squinted at her, clearly forming a mental picture, and then laughed.

"I think it would turn your hair entirely orange. Like a carrot."

"Oh, that wouldn't do at all."

Once they were through with fashion, their talk turned to other people. Kathleen's overbearing mother, the admirable if alarming gall of the professor, and Chago. Especially Chago. Kathleen thought he was exciting and dashing and colorful.

"A life with Chago wouldn't be boring," Teddy said, "but it would be also be dangerous."

The girl stirred her drink with the long spoon provided. "You don't seem to put up with boredom well yourself. You ran away from finishing school to become a nurse and travel the world. These are modern times, though, and girls get to have more fun. What would you do, if you were my age today? Would you be a nurse again, or would you marry?"

"I would be a nurse." Teddy didn't even have to think about it. "Too much focus is still put on a woman getting married, and not on her personal value."

The blonde grinned. "You mean you wouldn't latch onto Chago in a heartbeat?"

Teddy laughed and laughed. When she recovered herself, she said, "It's fun to flirt with young men when one knows nothing will come of it. Certainly less risky. I think our friend would be happier, though, with a more domestic sort. He leads an exciting life and needs a refuge. I don't think he realizes it yet."

"Oh." Kathleen looked disappointed.

"Don't despair. There are plenty of ambitious young men looking for an ally, rather than a refuge. But I need to change the subject," Teddy said. "You know that we're trying to find out who killed Mr. Janzen." "Aunt Helen didn't do it, if that's what you think. She hated him, but she wanted the watch more. She couldn't get it back if she didn't even know if he still had it."

"I believe you," Teddy said. "But we need to learn more about Raymond Janzen himself. You are old enough to remember the years he was close to your aunt and uncle. Did you meet him?"

"Yes, we visited often. I remember Ray. He was tall and dark-haired and full of exciting stories. I had a horrible crush on him."

This produced a smile. "You do like the rogues, don't you?"

"I stopped liking him after he ruined my uncle."

"Did you recognize him on the train?"

"Yes, although Aunt Helen turned away. I guess she thought he would recognize her. I sort of hoped he'd recognize me, but he didn't seem to. Not what a girl wants, to not be remembered."

"He thought of you as a little girl."

Kathleen's lips turned down. "I tried my best to make him think of me as more than that. I wore my prettiest dresses, even stole my mother's lipstick so I could put it on after we got to my aunt's house. I got a walloping for that later, but Ray thought it was cute. He said I looked like a girl he used to date."

Teddy's hand tightened on her drink. "Did he tell you about her?"

"Oh, I was mad with jealousy," she replied. "I wanted to know how old she was, where she lived, was she married to someone else, was she blonde like me—everything, so I'd know what he liked."

"What did he say?"

"He'd known her when he lived in Virginia, before the Great War. She had redder hair than mine, and she liked to hike in bloomers."

"Did he tell you her name?"

"No, he wouldn't, but I asked. He wouldn't say more than that, just that they'd broken up and that's why he went to war. I bet he lied about that, too!"

I bet he did.

Chapter 13

Monday morning came early, especially for Teddy. She hadn't gone dancing for a change, but both she and Cornelia had lain awake for hours, discussing what they'd learned and how to find out more. Plus, of course, what would happen if Cornelia's uncle were held over for trial. The professor had been thrown in jail many times in his youth, mostly for disturbing the peace with his inventions, but his bout with pneumonia had given his niece a good scare. Teddy thought privately that the elderly man wasn't quite as fragile as Cornelia thought, but she didn't want to be proven wrong.

Cornelia was up and dressed before Teddy had even finished washing her face. "Hurry; we need to leave for the arraignment," she announced, poking her head into the bathroom. "It's a good thing Uncle Percival brought a down payment; it may have to double as bail. At least if they let him have bail."

"They'll let him have bail, I'm sure," Teddy said soothingly. "I'll hurry." In the room across from theirs, she could hear movement—footsteps and the thump of suitcases. She wouldn't get to say goodbye to Kathleen, but they had exchanged addresses.

Once she was finished with her morning ablutions, she selected a dark blue suit from the wardrobe. Cornelia paced— or, rather, stomped—around their room while Teddy dressed.

"The sheriff may not have as much influence in deciding the charges as he would like," the older woman mused aloud. "If they charge Uncle Percival with murder, they could keep him locked up until Judge Bullock arrives next month."

Teddy adjusted her hose and stepped into her Mary Janes. She wondered if she would be permitted to put a dusting of makeup on her face. "In that case, we bring his attorney down here and make them set some sort of bail for him. He's not Al Capone."

"He may die before then." Cornelia was clenching her hands again. Poor thing, she was really fretting.

"Not with us to watch over him," Teddy said. "Why don't you go get Mitch?"

After Cornelia left, Teddy applied some powder and a little lipstick. The occasion was somber, but a good appearance never hurt a situation.

The sign on the outskirts of town proclaimed the population of Inverness as 1270. Cornelia was certain that there were more people than that crowded around the courthouse. The courthouse dome rose from a human sea that filled the town square and swallowed up the surrounding streets. Uncle Percival's arraignment must have been the most excitement the county had seen in quite some time.

Mitch leaned on the horn. Still, they crept a few feet, stopped, then edged a little further down the street. He got them as close as he could to the courthouse before giving up.

"Sorry, ladies," he said. "The crowd is twelve deep in every direction. We're going to have to hoof it from here." He pushed the driver side door open, dislodging the three men leaning against it.

By the time he reached Cornelia's door, the press had spotted them. Cameras flashed in their faces as the women climbed out of the car. Mitch moved between them and the closest reporters. The look in his eyes as he moved to Teddy's right side told Cornelia that Mitch took perverse pleasure in blocking his rivals' shots.

"Stick close to me Miss Theodora," he said, offering her his arm. "I'll make sure none of these goons trample you."

Cornelia frowned when Teddy draped herself around the proffered arm. Since when had either of them needed a protector?

152

Instead, she stepped in front of them. "Make way," Cornelia commanded, in a tone that would have made General Pershing step out of her way.

At least a dozen men leapt aside, making a path for her.

Mitch couldn't hide a grin when he saw a couple of the boys snap to attention as Cornelia marched past them toward the courthouse steps.

A young deputy stopped her at the door.

Cornelia glared at him. Her square jaw clamped tight.

He swallowed hard, but stood his ground. "The courthouse is full, ma'am," he said. "You'll have to wait outside."

"Don't be ridiculous," Cornelia snapped. "My uncle needs me to post bail."

"No offence, ma'am, but I've heard from about every sort of relative this morning. For a tin canner, the old guy's got more relatives here than about anybody I know."

"Young man, I don't know what sort of people you associate with, but I do not lie. I am Cornelia Pettijohn. Professor Percival Pettijohn is my uncle. Now either let us pass, or call your superior out here to identify us. Sheriff Bowden has spoken to us many times during his investigation."

The deputy hesitated for a second, and then stepped aside.

"Thank you," she said, as she opened the door.

Mitch and Teddy followed close behind.

Cornelia enjoyed seeing disappointment circulate through the gallery when the bailiff announced the presiding judge. It was the twentieth century! How could people still look for entertainment in the misery of others? Her uncle's arraignment was a huge letdown for the barbarians who had camped in front of the courthouse to be front row spectators. An audible groan rose because Circuit Judge Bullock had assigned the arraignment to the local probate judge. More disappointment followed when the county prosecutor's office sent a junior attorney to read a prepared affidavit.

When called upon, the bespectacled young lawyer stood. "Your Honor, after consulting with the sheriff's office, it is the people's considered opinion that..." he glanced down at the paper clenched in his hand, "Mr. Pettijohn is a material witness to and suspected participant in criminal activities."

"He means the old fossil's a murderer," a voice boomed from the back of the room.

The whole crowd erupted in roars of laughter and shouting, punctuated by the steady hammer of the judge's gavel.

The attorney gave up on reading the affidavit, unclenched his fists, and dropped the crumpled paper on his table. He stood for a moment with his back to the judge.

Cornelia watched him as he looked at the faces in the crowd. The silence lasted only a few seconds, but the sobering effect it had on the courtroom lingered. She wasn't sure who the youngster was, but he was no fool. When he was a little more seasoned, he would play the emotions of a jury the way she played her fiddle.

His voice jarred her from her thoughts.

"Your Honor, Mr. Pettijohn resides nearly a thousand miles from the great state of Florida. He is a man of considerable means, and has a known disregard for requests from local authorities. We must consider him a flight risk." The rather serious young prosecutor never glanced at her uncle, as he continued in the same quiet voice. "In light of the evidence, it would be foolhardy to not ask that Percival Pettijohn provide the court with a cash bond in sufficient amount to discourage him from leaving the county until the investigation is closed."

"Do you have anything to say for yourself, Mr. Pettijohn?"

"Your Honor, Sheriff Bowden is an honest man in a difficult job."

His voice no longer had the deep richness Cornelia remembered from her youth, but she could tell he was getting ready to spread a thick coat of horse manure around the courtroom.

154

"I have no ill will over spending my birthday locked in a six-by-four cell because I ventured a little too far from my hotel. Had I realized filming a few alligators in their natural surroundings would cause so much trouble, I would have stopped. Maybe then he and his deputies would have gotten around to investigating some real criminals."

He continued. "I'm offended that repeated attempts to break into my room were ignored. In light of the murders, it seems that the theft of my personal property by a pair of hoodlums is not all that important. Those hoodlums remain free to travel wherever they wished unmolested. They were only identified when my niece took action."

He turned and smiled at Teddy and Cornelia, then lifted his arm, pointing them out to the assembled gawkers. "These angels of mercy who gallantly braved the French trenches to tend our wounded in the Great War were here for me in my hour of need. They risked their lives to chase down criminals that the police couldn't be bothered with. While I was caged, these violent criminals robbed me and shot at my family."

After a dramatic pause, Professor Pettijohn turned to the judge. "Your Honor, as a visitor to your state, I am obliged to remember that I am *only* a visitor. Florida is not my home. All I ask is that the court takes into account that I am a guest in your home, reduced to the station of an unwelcome guest, and deprived of the freedom to leave."

The judge lowered his head.

Cornelia figured he was trying not to laugh. She had never seen her uncle spout so much hogwash.

"Professor Pettijohn, in the past twenty-four hours I have spoken at length with Sheriff Bowden, Kentucky law enforcement, the prosecutors' office, and Judge Bullock. You, sir, hold a place among the most intelligent men in the country. You also have an impressive reputation for causing trouble. The state would be remiss to allow you unfettered freedom. In the interest of justice, I am releasing you on a 1,000 dollar cash bond and your word of honor that you will not set one foot outside of Citrus County until this matter is resolved."

"Thank you, Your Honor."

Once the judge announced his decision, Tiny and Cesare rushed out of the courthouse. It wasn't like either of them had never been arraigned before, and they needed to beat the exiting crowd.

Tiny wished his last lawyer had been half as good at bushwa as the old geezer had been. He'd practically laid it down with a trowel. Tiny could've done without the 'hoodlum' part, but he'd been called worse.

They reached the car and Cesare took the driver's seat. They cruised to a spot where they could see when their mark left, and follow him home.

Cornelia shook her head in disbelief. Her uncle had to be the only person alive who could walk out of jail with the jailer carrying his bag. The old man slapped him on the back as he got into the car. "Now don't forget to stop by for supper before you folks head back up North," he said as he slung the professor's bag into the back of the black Cadillac. "My wife will fry you up a mess of snapper that will make your mouth think you're dining on manna from heaven."

"It will be our pleasure."

The professor's smile told her it would be *his* pleasure. She marveled at his ability to find enjoyment in the most unexpected places. He had been locked in that dreadful cage on his birthday instead of visiting the Million Dollar Pier as he had planned. He was keen to see this engineering marvel, but when his plans went awry Uncle Percival managed to befriend a small-town jailer who was holding him in custody.

"I am sure we can find time for another friendly game of checkers too, if you've a mind to get beaten again," the professor said as Teddy emerged from the jail's office.

"The party's on!" she announced. "Peter said he'd handle everything."

The trio piled into Mitch's car for the drive back to Homosassa. Cornelia settled into the back seat and took a small notebook from her bag. Her uncle chatted with their driver, but she kept her mouth shut on the way back to their hotel. There was no benefit in trying to chasten him. Every attempt to curb the irascible old coot's mischief provoked him into more tomfoolery. He lived his life as if every day was a grand adventure designed for his amusement.

She couldn't find any amusement in his current predicament. Didn't he realize someone was trying to frame him for murder? She busied herself thinking about the motives the other people on the Mullet Express had for wanting Mr. Janzen dead. There were too many possibilities. What she needed was a way to narrow the list. She and Teddy had already scratched Rowley; he had motive, but lacked the opportunity to poison Janzen. Besides, he wasn't at their hotel when that bottle of savin was planted in her uncle's room; Teddy had confirmed that with Mr. Hoyt. The killer was either someone staying at their hotel or one of the goons that kept trying to break into his room.

Before she had time to order her thoughts, they pulled up to the doors of the Homosassa Hotel.

Peter had moved quickly: a small crowd of greeters were in front of the grand hotel to welcome them. The Carsons, Chago, Peter Rowley, and several members of the staff filled the entrance. A porter opened the car door and assisted the professor to the curb. Chago helped Teddy out. Mitch tried to follow suit with Cornelia, but she waved him aside. "I'm fine. Will you be joining us after you park?"

The young man grinned. "If I'm invited."

"Yes, of course." She knew he was probably thinking of his story, but an extra pair of eyes might keep her uncle safer. Not everyone at his belated birthday party would wish him well. There was a murderer lurking somewhere among the partygoers.

She entered the hotel, and saw that Peter had taken charge of things. He was currently tying a blindfold on the professor. "Miss Cornelia, Miss Teddy, go ahead. I want him to get the full effect in one view - kapow!"

The ladies entered the ballroom to find it blanketed in orange and white banners. Tropical flowers decorated the tables, blazing creations in crimson, gold, tangerine, with touches of blue or purple. The centerpiece of the room was an enormous white cake studded with fresh orange slices. The sweet aroma made Cornelia's mouth water, and reminded her that she hadn't eaten since breakfast.

"Mr. Rowley has outdone himself," she said, admiring the straw boater hat that topped the enormous cake and the charming model train circling its base.

"This is utterly darling," Teddy gushed. "It was so nice of Peter to help arrange things in our absence."

"I think he hopes to make a good commission," Cornelia said, "but he is going to be disappointed." Her uncle hadn't come to Florida with the intent of buying property here, and probably wouldn't; this was merely where he could confront the man who had cheated him. Now, he was suspected of murder. They might celebrate today, but what would happen tomorrow?

"Here they come," Teddy said, breaking her brown study.

After the men walked in, Rowley removed the blindfold. Everyone shouted, "Happy birthday!"

The professor beamed at the display. "Marvelous! All this for me?"

"We need to outshine Saint Petersburg tonight," the land agent said. He gestured to the gallery, and the musicians broke into 'Bugle Call Rag'.

Tiny Belluchi loitered in the halls outside the grand ballroom of the new hotel. He had chosen his spot well, and moved into the shadows whenever a guest passed close to the alcove where he kept watch on the professor's party. Right now, the old man was the focus of all eyes, but as the party progressed, people would get distracted. Especially after imbibing the punch Wall's men had provided. The Cuban stepped into the hall, and Tiny retreated further, waiting until his counterpart had disappeared in the direction of the stairs.

Having one of Wall's men gone made it all the better for him. He sidled into the ballroom through one of the smaller doors; the party decorations provided some cover that way. People were chattering, but the music drowned out most of the talk. That'd be useful if the geezer put up a squawk.

158

Those old bags, the one built like a fire plug and the face stretcher, were talking to the land agent. Tiny's target was studying the cast-iron toy train with fascination.

Must be in his second childhood, Tiny thought.

When the women moved to the main entrance to greet newcomers, he approached the table. The blindfold had been discarded on a nearby tray; he picked it up, twisting the ends in his large fingers.

"Surprise," he said, stopping behind the old man. He dropped the fabric over his prey's eyes and tied it.

"Another one? Wonderful!" the geezer said, tucking the small black locomotive into his pocket.

Leading him to the side door and out of the ballroom was a piece of cake. Tiny had the old guy stuffed into his Ford before anyone knew he was gone. He nodded to his compatriots crouched behind another flivver. If anyone followed in pursuit, they were gonna get their own surprise.

"I can't believe a charming man like you isn't married," Teddy said, her hand on Peter's arm. "Handsome, a veteran, a hard worker, dedicated to selling land..."

Peter flushed, and not from the punch. "I hope to establish myself first, Miss Lawless. I'm not just a land agent, I'm a customer. You know that private fishing lodge down on the river? I'm looking to get the money up to build my own lodge nearby, for hunting and fishing."

That made a fair bit of sense to Cornelia. There were plenty of waterfowl here for the taking, if one avoided the alligators. "So you intend to host sportsmen coming down here to hunt?"

"Not just host them; be their guide. I've got a good-sized boat I restored and I've hunted here my entire life. I know all the good spots, and nothing tastes better than food you've caught yourself."

"Including alligators?" Teddy asked.

"It's good fried," Peter replied, and they laughed.

Listening to this, Cornelia thought of a way her uncle could apologize to her for his deceit. Helping the young man who had rescued them achieve his dream would be excellent, and much more satisfying than an apology after the fact.

She glanced around the room, looking for her uncle, but didn't see him. Strange; he was normally very hard to miss.

As she searched the crowd, Mitch arrived and joined them. "Hey, great setup!"

Peter frowned. "Aren't you one of the drivers for the Company?"

"We engaged him for the day," Teddy said, "and he's our extra man for the party."

"That's me, Mister Extra," the reporter quipped.

The music started again and Peter asked Teddy to dance. She must have seen the concern in Cornelia's face, because she hesitated. "What's wrong?"

"I don't see Uncle Percival. I thought he was playing with the train, but he seems to have gone elsewhere."

"Perhaps he needed to visit the water closet," Teddy suggested.

That was logical, but Cornelia wasn't so sure. There were a number of people who would profit if something bad happened to her uncle.

"Perhaps I should check," Mitch said.

Mitch, the designated water closet checker, found no one inside. When they made a sweep of the lobby, Chago came thundering down the stairs and shouted in Spanish to his companions.

"*Las habitaciones están vacías. Los hombres se han ido.*"

The rooms are empty. The men are gone.

Cornelia's stomach clenched. "They have him. Let's go!"

A heavy dark car was leaving the hotel driveway. Chago and his men were crowding the door in their haste. The two women prepared to follow them out with Mitch, but stopped at the sound of gunfire. Shrieks followed.

Mitch peered through the tall arched window. "Those torpedoes are Antinori's; I'd bet my rent on it."

A surge of screaming guests, clutching cigarettes and hand fans, poured in through the front doors. Wall's men fanned out to the sides of the lobby, where there was a little more cover, and returned fire.

"We need to get out there," Cornelia shouted, above the sound of breaking glass and general uproar. "Otherwise, we'll never catch them."

Mitch gaped. "Are you nuts? It's a war zone out there."

"We're not the main targets. Remember the trenches? Stay low." She scuttled down the hall, Teddy close behind.

"Oh, applesauce!" Mitch fell in line.

The left wing of the hotel had a smaller entrance. Cornelia scanned the lawn and lot. She spotted three men crouched behind a sedan. One popped up above the hood and fired another shot into the lobby. The response was quick and loud.

The old nurse took advantage of the distraction to drop behind a row of decorative bushes. She scuttled along the line toward the parking lot. The branches clutched at her, scratching her head and shoulder, then sprang back to confront the next intruder.

"Ow ow ow," was Teddy's response, while Mitch opted to mutter obscenities.

When they arrived at the edge of the building, she decided to risk poking her head above the foliage. Two of the invaders were looking for targets in the lobby windows, while the third was changing guns. There was, perhaps, fifteen feet of open space between them and the first parked car.

"Go!" She charged from the bushes and ran for it, followed by her companions. The air was sharp with the scent of gunpowder, and they were running for cover. *Just like the trenches.* Cornelia fought a shudder.

The man changing guns spotted them. "Hey! Get outta here!" He raised his weapon, but was brought down by a shot from behind the trio. Chago was at the exit they'd just left.

They snaked between the vehicles until they reached Mitch's. Cornelia slid into the driver's seat. She pushed the starter button and the Cadillac vibrated with life.

A hand shot in and grabbed her arm. "It's my car. Let me drive." Mitch shouted.

"Get in the other side and prepare to shoot," she snapped, pulling his gun out of the car door's side pocket. She slapped the butt in his palm.

Mitch stared at her, nodded, and ran around to the other side.

Teddy threw herself onto the back seat, gasping for air. "Not...again."

"Hang on!" Cornelia shouted, and they were off.

They reached the Dixie Highway, and Cornelia hesitated. North or south?

"Turn right," the reporter said. "They'd head for Tampa."

She jerked the wheel to the right and stomped on the gas.

As she made the turn, though, another vehicle shot out from the other side of the highway, from the promised Great White Way, with the sound of a siren. She jerked the steering wheel hard, but the heavy frame of the Cadillac still slammed into the side of the sheriff's vehicle. She could hear the wood splinter inside the body of the car.

Was the driver Andy Davidson, or Sheriff Bowden himself? Cornelia didn't take the time to look. She threw the car in reverse. Her turn was so sharp, Teddy slid to the opposite side of the back seat.

"Hang on again," Cornelia yelled. She slammed her foot on the accelerator, and they lurched forward.

Behind them, an Oldsmobile also made the turn, fishtailing in the shells.

"We've lost them," Teddy moaned from the back. "The shootout cost us too much time."

"Not yet," Mitch said. "There aren't many turnoffs ahead. But zikes! The car! I'll be paying for the repairs out of my paycheck."

"Don't worry about your car. See if you can spot theirs." Cornelia said. She gritted her teeth and leaned forward, willing the Cadillac to move faster.

The city disappeared quickly behind the trees at the perimeter of the developed town. Soon, clouds of dust and ground shells floating above the road told them that they were getting close. The wail of the siren behind them was nearly drowned out by the roar of motors and wheels echoing through the trees. She wasn't sure she wanted to know who was cranking the siren. Whoever it was would probably arrest all of them when this chase ended. Not that it mattered. She would rather be thrown under the jail than let these gangsters hurt her uncle.

Then, Cornelia caught sight of Tiny Belluchi's Ford. The driver of the Olds must have spotted it at the same time, because it veered left to go around her. She stood on the accelerator, but the Olds passed them anyway. Soon, the Ford and the Olds were vying for the same share of road. Sparks flew as they collided, spattering her windshield with dust and paint chips.

Mitch grabbed the edge of the roof through the open window and pulled his upper torso up and out of it. He braced his shoulder against the back edge of the door frame. "Go left!" he shouted.

"Don't shoot at the passengers!" she ordered. "Aim for the wheels!"

"Got it!" He fired, gripping the gun with both hands. The kick knocked him awry, but Teddy grabbed his jacket before he could tumble out.

Ahead of them, each vehicle attempted to push the other off the road at speeds that were unsafe for the best of highways. Dust and flying pieces of shell made it difficult to tell whether one had an advantage over the other. The Oldsmobile was heavier, but whoever was behind the steering wheel of the Ford knew how to drive. She would have appreciated his skill more if her uncle were not his prisoner.

Cornelia swore as a large chunk of seashell hit the window just above the steering wheel, fracturing the glass. Lines ran in all directions, further restricting visibility. "You'll have to do better than that to stop me," she shouted, flooring the Cadillac and ramming the Ford from behind.

Mitch groaned.

"Pipe down," Cornelia snapped, ramming the Ford again. "We've got him boxed in. Take out one of his tires."

Mitch braced himself again and fired three shots in quick succession. At least one of them hit its mark, sending the Ford careening toward the swamp and dragging the front bumper of the Oldsmobile with it. The cloud of blue smoke and the scent of burning rubber told her that only a strong foot on the brakes was keeping the rest of the Olds out of the swamp.

Cornelia pulled to the side of the road and stopped behind the Oldsmobile. Chago and his companion Salvador emerged from it. The siren gave one last half-scream as the sheriff's car pulled up beside them. The light was starting to fade, but she could still see the anger lining Bowden's face.

Before either of them said a word, the door of the Ford opened and Tiny folded himself out of the wrecked car - shotgun in hand - and let out a scream, followed by a string of curses. His shotgun slipped from his fingers and splashed into the brackish water. Tiny cursed again.

There was a loud sucking noise as the large man wrenched one big foot from the muck and took another step toward solid ground. He didn't scream quite as loud but the string of curses grew longer with each step he took.

Sheriff Bowen got out of his car and waited, gun drawn, for the big man to lumber to the bank. There was no need to wade into the swamp after him; nobody could run in a swamp full of black mangroves.

About halfway to shore, the swamp claimed one of his shoes. Tiny whimpered, looking from the car to the Sheriff and back again.

Cesare was no help. From the interior of the car, they could hear a different group of curses. The back seat passenger was pummeling his other captor with something block-shaped and black. Cesare flung open the door on his side. "*Basta!* Enough! I surrender already!"

Mitch took pity on Tiny. He pulled a thick blanket from under the seat and walked over to the edge of the swamp. "This won't make it easy to walk through the pencil roots, but it should keep them from ripping your ankles to shreds," he said, as he shook out the blanket and spread it over the water.

Tiny took one careful step, winced and took another.

Just as he collapsed on the bank, a car pulled in beside the sheriff's, windows open.

Cornelia heard the unmistakable sound of a pump action shotgun being racked.

"We don't want trouble, Sheriff," the graveled voice of the weapon's owner boomed. "Just lay your gun on the ground and stand there nice and quiet. The rest of you mugs do the same."

Bowden hesitated, and a second shotgun racked.

He laid his gun on the ground.

"Wise choice, Sheriff," one of the men said. "We don't want anybody to get hurt."

"What do you want, then?"

"Now that's not a nice way to talk to a couple of peace lovin' citizens. Joe and me came all the way from Ybor City to bring the birthday boy's movin' picture to his party. The boss had it developed for him as a special gift."

Sheriff Bowden's eyes widened. "*You* have the professor's film?"

There was a deep chuckle. "We do, but it seems the party's moved. Can't say much about the location, but watchin' Tiny squirm makes for some fine entertainment."

The passenger side door opened briefly, then closed again. "This ain't the most exciting picture show I've seen, but the boss thinks you'll enjoy some of the more interesting moments. We'll just leave it right here on the shoulder and be on our way."

Shells ground again as the car wheeled backwards at an angle, then turned south. It roared into life, and sped away. A brown paper parcel sat beside the road. For a few seconds they all stared at the package, then rushed to claim the prize.

Tiny didn't make it far. Knowing how angry Leo was going to be kept him going, but walking thirty-odd feet through brackish swamp water and black mangrove spikes had taken its toll on him. He hated Florida.

Chapter 14

That evening, Mitch drove the film maker and his nurses to the Homosassa Hotel for a private viewing of the film. Cornelia's uncle was too excited to stay still. He took out his pocket watch and checked it against the one above the hotel desk, then walked back to the door to see if Sheriff Bowden was in the parking lot.

"He's late," the professor grumbled.

"By two minutes."

The sheriff's arrival saved them from another lecture on punctuality.

"I've made all the arrangements with the manager," Bowden said. "He's going to let us have one of the drawing rooms."

Cornelia nodded. There was no need to ask for details about the case; those were all over New and Old Homosassa. She had been pummeled with questions about the car chase and kidnapping when she returned to her hotel. Everyone there knew that Tiny Belluchi's automobile had to be pulled from the swamp and that he and Cesare were arrested on the spot.

At dinner, every conversation in town was about the sheriff, the professor's movie, the kidnapping, and city boys who didn't have the good sense to stay put when they landed in a Florida bayou. By dessert, they knew that between the black mangroves and mussel shells, Mr. Belluchi's feet had taken quite a battering. The sheriff had to send for the town doctor, who was now available. Word was, Tiny would be lucky if he didn't have to attend his arraignment in a wheelchair.

During the ladies' meal at the Riverside Lodge, Susie relayed news of how the deputy sent to the hotel to bring Mazzi in arrived too late. Leo had checked out long before the lawman arrived, and nobody knew where he'd gone. The sheriff had men searching, of course, but when a man like Leonardo Mazzi didn't want to be found, the odds of locating him were pretty slim.

The room the concierge led them into was set up for a small party, not a criminal investigation. Comfortable chairs were positioned with good views of the screen, and two low tables held trays of cheese, crackers, and petit-fours within easy reach of the guests.

"Would you prefer ice water or coffee for the viewing?" the young man asked.

They looked at one another. "Both," the professor said. "Thank you for your hospitality."

After Edward left, the sheriff grinned. "Best appointed office I ever had. I could solve all my crimes if I had a place like this."

The beverages arrived with the projectionist. The hotel had stipulated that a trained employee run their equipment; Bowden had stipulated that the man be of trustworthy character and sworn to secrecy. The latter was amenable to everyone involved.

"I can't wait to see how the mountains in Tennessee came out," Teddy said.

"You'll need to wait a little longer," the professor said. "The sheriff is only interested in the rolls I've shot since we arrived in Florida."

"But I want to see what my new winter coat looks like on film."

"As do I," said Uncle Percival, "since it was my gift. But the sheriff is more concerned with content than style."

The projectionist dimmed the lights in the theater. A moment later, the screen lit up with the featured film for a very select group.

A black-and-white Teddy stood beside a sign reading, "Welcome to Florida". She smiled and gestured to the words.

On the other side stood a stolid Cornelia with one hand on her hip.

"Gray hair and dress," the professor said. "You don't suffer much from lack of color, Corny."

Cornelia resisted the urge to kick him in the shin.

"How long do you think it will be before the film gets to Homosassa, sir?"

"Not long, Sheriff. There was the stop in Gainesville, then the shots I took in Ocala when we made our unexpected visit. After that comes some film of the Mullet Express."

"You'll want to pay close attention to that part," Teddy said. "Cornelia captured the fight on film."

"That might be of evidentiary use," Bowden said. He turned in his seat to the projectionist. "Is there a way to move faster to that part of the movie?"

"Yes, sir." The room darkened while the young man worked with the reel. "Let's try this."

Cornelia recognized the hotel from Ocala. Teddy posed again, this time clasping a sun hat to her curls. Peter Rowley stood nearby with an amused expression on his face.

"You're getting close," the professor said. "That was Sunday."

"Should I try going further up?"

"Not a good idea," Pettijohn said. "You're likely to overshoot."

They watched silently through several minutes of posing and panning. Uncle Percival seemed to like doing long left-to-right shots.

Now the train dominated the screen. The camera eye began at the dark engine with wisps of steam emanating from its body, then shifted to the passenger cars and its tiny windows, and finally to the baggage car and caboose. Suddenly, they were looking at the professor's back as he approached the conductor.

"What's this?"

"That's where Cornelia took over, Professor." Teddy watched as her film counterpart posed, then hiked her skirt. "Oh, dear. I didn't mean to show so much of my knees. Will that prejudice the court?"

Bowden chuckled. "I don't think so, ma'am. Many girls visiting the beach show more than that. Of course, the beach censors frequently escort them off the beach if the suit is more than six inches above the knee."

"That doesn't seem fair."

"Young men get the same treatment for when they show up in those new suits with removable vests. People in Florida want to take their children to the beach. We don't cotton to topless swimming. We've had so many local ordinances passed, that the state is considering new legislation regulating beachwear."

"Look!" the projectionist shouted. "The fight's started!"

They all leaned forward, watching Hofstetter and the dead man exchange blows. It was more dramatic to Cornelia than the tiny view through the camera had been. She watched the crowd gathering soundlessly, the railmen dropping their loads and running to the battle. Mouths moved, but nothing was audible.

The men were pulled apart. The conductor spoke to each of them, but no words could be heard.

"I wish this had sound," Bowden said.

"I can read lips," Teddy said. "They didn't want the police called."

"Nor did Mr. Janzen desire to swear a complaint," the professor added.

Bowden gave them both the stinkeye. "That should be easy to confirm with the conductor."

The camera's eye made another trip along the train.

"There's Rowley getting in the back car," the professor said. "It doesn't look like he was anywhere near Janzen. I remain the chief suspect."

"I'm not so sure of that," Cornelia said, staring at the figures near the baggage car. "Could you pause the film?"

The projectionist nodded and did what he was asked.

Cornelia stood up and moved closer to the screen.

"What are you looking at Miss Pettijohn?" Bowden asked.

"That," she said, pointing to the figures near the baggage car. "Do you recognize it?"

170

Bowden got up and walked over to where she was standing. He stared at the screen for a moment and then let out a long low whistle. "I'll be a goose's uncle. I wouldn't have expected that."

"Are we finished?" the projectionist asked, after watching the sheriff study the film from different angles.

Sheriff Bowden didn't seem to hear him. "It isn't proof, you know."

Cornelia nodded. "But..."

Bowden held up one hand. "I'm not arguing with you, Miss Pettijohn, but by itself it's not enough. Unless you've got pictures of the two of them together, a good lawyer would make sure a jury never sees your uncle's film."

"Sheriff," the projectionist said.

"No, we are not finished. You can start the film again when Miss Pettijohn and I are back in our seats." Then he turned to the professor. "That is, if the scene you described on the loading platform is on this reel."

"No that was two reels later."

"Then let's load that one."

The projectionist looked at the stack of film canisters and back at them. "Which reel am I looking for?"

"The one that starts with the alligators," the professor said.

The young man opened one canister, unrolled a foot or so of film, and held it up to the light. He frowned, set that reel aside and opened the next one. Two attempts later he found the professor's gators and laced them into the projector.

After a moment or two of watching alligators snap at each other and chase the cheeky pelicans that tried to horn in on their fish-head feast, the sheriff asked him to move ahead to the train footage.

Any doubts about the accuracy of the professor's memory were banished by his movie. The film played out the body dump exactly as he had described when he was sitting in the Crystal River Jail. Sheriff Bowden alternated between watching the familiar story unfold on screen and casting puzzled looks at the professor.

When the reel ended, the sheriff took Cornelia aside. "Your uncle confuses me, ma'am. I can understand the need to focus on what you're doing. My boys used to drive me to distraction when I was trying to work on a report. But this is a murder. How can you see and not notice a murder twenty feet away?"

"I've asked myself similar questions many times. There's no answer," she replied. "Sometimes I think he was born blessed with luck because God knew he needed more than his fair share to keep from wandering into traffic."

The sheriff chuckled.

"What are you going to do now?" Cornelia asked.

"Since Cesare and Tiny are already in custody for kidnapping, I don't imagine it will be hard to add a murder charge."

"What about their boss, Leo Mazzi?"

"Arresting Mr. Mazzi is easier said than done. He hasn't been seen since our adventure earlier today."

The projectionist handed the sheriff the stack of film canisters. "The two reels you watched are on top."

"Thanks. If you'll excuse me, Miss Pettijohn, the prosecutor will have my hide if I don't get these locked up before I go home."

Deputy Andy arrived at Cornelia's door the following morning with his hat in one hand and a note from the sheriff in the other. "I hope I didn't wake you, ma'am."

"Young man, I'm used to rising early. The army doesn't have much use for layabouts."

His ears turned pink. "The sheriff asked me to bring you this." He handed her the note and stood waiting while she read.

Miss Pettijohn,
Dani Hegstad was picked up last night in Jacksonville, trying to board a northbound train. My son left to pick him

*up as soon as we were notified. He believes they will be back
in Inverness by noon.*

If you're still willing to translate, I could use help.
- Bowden

"Tell him I will be in his office at noon."

"Thanks Ma'am."

As soon as the deputy left, Cornelia woke Teddy. "I'm
going down to the desk and call Mitch. Would you like to have
breakfast with me before I leave?"

Teddy sat up. "I thought you were going bird watching
this morning. Did the birds sleep in?"

Cornelia handed Teddy the note.

"Oh. How exciting. Can I watch you grill the suspect?"

"I'm not grilling anyone. I'm just going to help the boy
understand the sheriff's questions and the sheriff understand
his answers. It will probably be dreadfully boring."

Teddy rested her hand on Cornelia's knee. "No, dear.
Listening to your uncle tell us what he filmed was boring. In
comparison, this will be quite thrilling."

Cornelia had to concede the point. It took all her
willpower to stay awake through his monologues.

"You can come if you want, but it is going to be a long
day. When the train gets back, I intend to locate that baggage
man. He may know more than he thinks about Mr. Janzen's
demise."

"Don't you think the sheriff will question him?'

"Of course he will, but it is not his family in trouble. I
want to find what he knows for myself."

This was the second night in a row that the projectionist
had come in to show the old coot's movie. At least it was
earlier and there was only one canister of film this time.
Sheriff Bowden had explained exactly where he wanted the
film to start. Meanwhile, several more seats were being
arranged for the viewing. Aside from the hotel staff, only
Sheriff Bowden and one of the locals were in the room.

He wiped the sweat from his palms on the front of his
vest and opened the film canister. It only took a moment to

find the scene the sheriff wanted and lace it into the projector. When he was done, he nodded to Bowden. The sheriff got up and opened the door. Thankfully, he also turned on the big overhead fan. The whir of the electric motor and the gentle breeze calmed his nerves. He wasn't sure why he was nervous; maybe it was the way the sheriff and his companion watched those entering the room. It was like thunderclouds building over the river. The air was charged. Sooner or later, the storm was going to break.

First, the professor came in, followed closely by the two women that always hovered around the old gent. The deputy that had been hanging around the hotel for the past week followed them in and shut the door.

Nobody was talking.

He wiped his hands again, then took out his handkerchief and wiped the beads of sweat from his forehead. The waiters had set up a nice spread, but he knew better than to help himself to a tall glass of sweet tea. The hospitality was for the guests.

A couple of new people arrived. The old guy smiled and greeted them like this was just a normal gathering. The newcomers were friendly enough, but the gent with Bowden was watching everyone.

The man nodded.

Bowden, standing next to him, asked, "Could you swear to it?"

He took a moment to think about it. "Yeah. Will I have to?"

"If it goes to court." Bowden put a hand on his shoulder. "Maybe it won't come to that."

The stranger nodded again, then took a seat in the back row.

Chapter 15

The projector whirred, and the scene at the station with Teddy mugging for the camera began. Rosemary Carson tittered at the poses she struck.

Cornelia leaned close to Mrs. Carson. "Watch this next part very closely. I shot it myself." On the screen, Pettijohn walked toward the train's engine. The focus shifted, panning at first, then was interrupted by a violent jerk to the scene of the fight. Janzen and Hofstetter circled, locked in a black-and-white battle. Hofstetter made his vicious uppercut and Rosemary gave a soft gasp, raising her hand to her mouth, as Janzen crumpled. Once again, Cornelia watched as the railroad staff broke up the fight, sending each combatant to a separate railcar.

The view shifted. Some travelers climbed into the passenger cars while others lagged behind, fanning themselves in a climate warmer than the one they'd dressed for. The camera's eye continued, resting on the baggage car now. Men hoisted suitcases and sacks of mail through the open door, stopping briefly to let one man out. That man jumped to the ground, carrying a flowered carpetbag in one hand. A female figure, approaching from the passenger area, thanked him noiselessly before opening it. After a brief search, she pulled out a medicine bottle and returned the bag to the man. He climbed back into the baggage car.

"Stop there," Cornelia told the projectionist. "Did you recognize anyone in the scene, Mrs. Carson?"

Rosemary Carson rose, and went to the refreshment table to fetch a glass of tea.

Cornelia joined her there. "Well?"

"Yes, I recognized a number of people. Your uncle, Teddy, and, of course, the men in the fight."

"Did you see yourself?"

"Me?" Her brow furrowed as she examined the screen. "Oh! You mean at the luggage car? That was me?"

"Indeed it was. The man standing in the doorway was the gentleman that helped you recover one of your bags before departure. You told him that you'd left your aspirin in your luggage, and the sun was giving you a headache."

"Yes, I did. I'd forgotten that. My, I do need to lose weight. I didn't realize how heavy I'd gotten."

"There's nothing wrong with your figure." Teddy had already forgotten her promise to keep quiet. "Winter clothing is just very thick."

"No more talk of women's figures, Teddy," Cornelia snapped. "Back to the point. Do you have that bottle now?"

"That particular bottle? No," Rosemary said, looking wary. "I threw it away after I took the last of the aspirin. The sun is very intense."

"I understand. Teddy is also very sensitive to the sun, and has taken a great deal of aspirin since we arrived."

Teddy made a face.

Cornelia didn't acknowledge it. "As a nurse, I'm familiar with the packaging of many medicines. It's a bottle, not a box, so probably not a powder. A tablet, then, but not Bayer. What brand was it?"

"Brand? I have no idea," Mrs. Carson said. "I picked it up while we traveled. I didn't pay much attention to the brand, I was simply happy to have some."

"Mmm-hmm. When did you first take some of these particular tablets?"

"I don't remember. Maybe the second day on the train to Jacksonville."

"And when did you finish off the medication?"

"Why does this matter?" She turned to Bowden. Her hands were balled up, and she opened them quickly. "Am I being charged with a crime, Sheriff? I heard that the poisoned man had been killed by his binder boy for the cash. Or are you referring to the man stuffed in the barrel and loaded onto the train? My husband can attest that I couldn't even lift my own trousseau when we were married."

"No, ma'am. I want to interview you as a potential witness. Or even as a fellow victim."

She started to retort, then paused at the meaning of his last words. "Victim?"

He nodded. "We have taken Dani Hegstad into custody. When his employer died, he feared that he would be arrested. He might even be accused of the poisoning. Mr. Janzen had purposely hired someone unfamiliar with English in order to freely conduct his unsavory business practices, but the boy was able to figure out that he was working with a crook. So, he took the money and fled."

The sheriff paused before continuing. "During questioning, though, he told us that you had been most solicitous to Raymond Janzen after the incident with Mr. Hofstetter. He was understandably sore after the blows he received. You were kind enough to offer him some aspirin from your purse."

"Oh." Rosemary looked down at her glass of tea, searching it as if her next answer could be found in its dregs. Alas, the hotel used Tetley bags.

"The lad said that his boss became ill shortly after. They both blamed it on the fight at the time."

The sheriff tilted his head to catch her eye, causing his moustache to droop in interesting ways. "Dr. Duffy, who attended the victim in his final hours, informed us that it was poison. I spoke to the medical examiner in Tampa, and he confirmed that Mr. Janzen was poisoned with savin."

"Savin? What is that?" The middle-aged woman feigned curiosity, but she didn't quite master the expression.

Not someone accustomed to lying, Cornelia thought. She took no pleasure in providing the explanation.

"There is no legal medical use for savin tablets." She drew herself up until her spine was ramrod-straight. "It does have an illegal one; to promote an abortion."

"Abortion?"

"Miscarriage is a less clinical term. Savin may cause a miscarriage, but it does as a byproduct of its poisoning the user."

"What does this have to do with me?" Rosemary asked. "You said that I was a witness, or even a victim. Of this—savin?"

Bowden retook the helm. "My deputies have checked the restaurant where Janzen and Hegstad had lunch before boarding the train. No one else became ill, and Dr. Duffy assures me that the reaction to savin begins fairly quickly."

"The only other substance he ingested was your aspirin," Cornelia added. "Uncle Percival offered him a drink from his flask, but Mr. Janzen was already ill by then. That's why I was asking you about the brand and when you'd taken the tablets. They may be the source of the poison."

"Oh." Rosemary's shoulders dropped and she half-smiled. She pulled a folded fan from her bag and opened it. "It is terribly warm in here."

Cornelia watched the woman try to dry the sweat on her forehead. Her heart ached with pity; this was merely a pause before the true harrowing began. She looked at Bowden. He took a gulp of ice water, ignoring them both for the moment.

Rosemary eventually broke the silence. The woman probably couldn't stand it. "Thank you for your concern. I understand why you were so interested."

"I've tried to remember the different times I've seen you over the past week," Cornelia said. "I don't recall your being ill, which was your good fortune."

"No. But wait—there was a canteen he drank from. Perhaps Mr. Hegstad or, perhaps, even Mr. Hofstetter added something to his libation."

"Unlikely," Bowden said. "When Dr. Duffy contacted us about the potential poisoning, we impounded the canteen of water. I asked that the doctor examine them, and he told me there was no telltale scent of the savin. I reckon I'll send it in for full testing, though."

Another silence. The sheriff heaved a sigh and took up the reins of the interrogation.

"Mrs. Carson. Are you positive that a search of your possessions wouldn't turn up the bottle?"

"Now see here," her husband said. "There is no call for you to go digging about in my wife's unmentionables."

Rosemary's shoulders went up again. "Why would you search them?"

"Miss Pettijohn has brought some irregularities to my attention. They led to my making some phone calls to Virginia and St. Augustine."

Rosemary turned to Cornelia. The look of betrayal in her eyes pierced like a glass shard. "What did you tell him?"

Cornelia met her gaze directly. She deserved that much. "You told me that your sister had died in the epidemic of 1918, and you named your daughter, born during the summer, after her. On another occasion, though, your husband remarked that your daughter was eight-and-a-half. She was born in 1917, not 1918."

"I must have made a mistake. Margaret died of influenza of the stomach; I guess I thought it was the Spanish Flu in 1918. It was so long ago."

"Must you put my wife through this, sheriff?" William Carson said. "You have nothing but a lot of speculation from a spinster with an overactive imagination."

Teddy broke in. "There is nothing imaginary about savin poisoning. The medical term for your sister's illness is gastroenteritis. That is also the most visible symptom of savin. We've seen its effects before."

"Bringing things to the point," Bowden said, "I have been thorough in investigating Miss Pettijohn's suspicions. I contacted the Reverend Archibald Janzen in St. Augustine... Raymond Janzen's father. Mr. Rowley was of some assistance in letting us know where he was from. After breaking the news of his son's death, I learned that Janzen had attended Washington and Lee in Lexington, Virginia. I believe that's where your family also resides."

"Yes," Rosemary muttered. The fan lay on the table in front of her, forgotten. Her forehead glowed with perspiration.

Her husband put an arm around her shoulders and drew her close. "We have little connection to the college. My wife and I had never met Janzen—that is, until this trip."

"Perhaps not, Mr. Carson, but can you say the same of your late sister-in-law? Mr. Janzen was a student at Washington and Lee from 1915 to 1917. Then, he was seized by a sudden fit of patriotism, and left school to serve in the Great War. His father thought it was most unlike him."

The sheriff glanced over to where the railman had retreated. "According to Mr. Rowley, some sort of trouble with a woman was involved."

Her reply was a long exhalation that ended in a hiss. "Can't you leave this alone?"

"No, I can't," he said softly, "Whatever my personal opinion of the man, my duty is to investigate his murder." Bowden's voice was barely above a whisper. "Mrs. Carson. I've called the authorities in Lexington to request the date and circumstances of your sister's death. Must I also make inquiries of her friends and other members of your family about more personal information?"

"No!" She slapped her palms on the table so hard that several petit-fours leapt from the plate. "Leave them alone! I'll answer your questions."

"Rosemary," her husband pleaded. "Stop and let me call our attorney."

Tears rolled down her face.

"Your sister knew Mr. Janzen," the sheriff said.

"Yes, to her great misfortune. She told me how charming, how handsome he was. She hoped he would propose marriage soon. Her friend Sissy would be her maid of honor, and I would be the matron." Her face was wet, and not only from sweat.

"She was fine at Easter. The next Sunday, Sissy came to fetch me when I was dressing Billy for church. Meg was ill, very ill. She'd been vomiting for two days and wouldn't see a doctor. Sissy hoped I could talk some sense into her."

"And did you go to your sister?" Cornelia knew that, one way or the other, it had already been too late to help Meg.

"She looked dead. Dead, but still able to speak. She was too weak to keep me from calling the doctor, but she refused to answer his questions. I got it out of her later. Meg thought she was... Must I say it?"

Bowden cleared his throat. This type of talk evidently embarrassed him. "Perhaps, Mrs. Carson, we can just skip to what your sister did."

"She told Mr. Janzen about it. She thought her darling Ray would do the right thing. He'd already done the wrong thing, so I don't know why she thought he would help her then. She wanted a ring. He gave her a bottle instead. Medication to regulate the female cycle."

"Savin," Cornelia said.

"Yes. I showed it to our family doctor, and he said that there was little hope of survival. I swore him to secrecy and we nursed her ourselves, Sheriff. Meg didn't want our parents to learn the truth. I didn't, either. So I watched my sister die in agony."

"You were very brave," Teddy said, dabbing her eyes.

"What happened afterward?" Bowden asked.

"The doctor was kind enough to tell my parents that it sounded like a digestive illness, based on my description. The illness had been swift, and no one realized how serious it was until she died. Meg was young, and everyone assumed that she would recover."

Rosemary dried her eyes on the handkerchief her husband handed her.

"The doctor couched his words very carefully when he broke the news to our parents. Mother blamed Sissy till the day she died for not having the doctor in sooner. Sissy endured it, rather than telling her the truth."

Teddy reached over, squeezed her hand. "I am so very sorry. You did the right thing—not telling her, that is."

"Begging your pardon, ladies, but we need to return to the present," Bowden said. "You took a bottle out of your luggage. What did it contain?"

"The rest of the pills that scoundrel gave my sister. I moved them to an empty aspirin bottle before I left Virginia."

"Rosemary, please stop!"

"I'm sorry, darling," she said to her husband. "That man destroyed Meg. Then he killed her. I had to do something."

"I understand," William Carson said gently.

"Do you?" She searched his face.

Bowden shifted from foot to foot as he tried to avoid looking directly at the Carsons. "It sounds like you knew Mr. Janzen was here before you came down, ma'am."

"I did. Sissy's husband got an advertisement with his picture. He remembered the man from Washington and Lee, and showed it to her. She showed it to me and... and I was incensed. Him, all smiles and success in his expensive suit. My sister, dead and disgraced."

Premeditated. Cornelia wished that the poor woman would stop talking, stop making it worse for herself, but Rosemary continued.

"I wrote to him under my married name, gave him my cousin's address in Norfolk. Arranged for a meeting here at the hotel. I requested a lunch meeting, to give me the chance to slip the pills into his coffee or sandwich, perhaps. As it turns out, I didn't need to go to the trouble. Someone else he'd wronged gave me the opportunity sooner."

"That would be Mr. Hofstetter," Bowden said.

"Yes. It was easier than I thought, putting a sweet smile on my face and offering pity to him for his injuries. We'd never met. I am not sure he knew Meg had a sister, so he didn't think twice about washing my headache pills down with the water in his canteen. I sat in the other railcar, where I was less likely to become a suspect, but oh, how I wish I could have watched as it began to work."

"I... if you say so, ma'am." Bowden looked away, his moustache dipping low.

Rosemary turned to Cornelia. "You and your friend helped care for him. Tell me... was he in much pain? Did he die in agony? I hope so."

"Rest assured," the nurse replied, "the savin lost little potency over the years."

"Good. Meg can rest in peace now."

Chapter 16

Cornelia thought about the murdered man she'd met on the Mullet Express as Mitch drove her to Inverness. Raymond Janzen was already condemned to death and his execution had begun before they met. It was impossible for her to feel sorry for him, now that the sordid story of his life was laid out. If ever a man needed killing...Cornelia didn't follow that thought any further. Everything she knew about him was secondhand. Such stories... fraud, theft, murder, treason... the latter cut deep.

If only Rosemary Carson had left Uncle Percival out of the crime. That was another path she hesitated to follow. Would she have let Rosemary get away with murder? Would she feel less guilty about ferreting out the truth?

She *did* feel guilty. When it came to Rosemary Carson's arrest, the blame fell on her shoulders. Rosemary had committed premeditated murder and tried to place the blame on Uncle Percival. She gave no thought to the consequences of her actions, no thought to what she was doing to her husband and children. Cornelia had done nothing wrong, but she wallowed in guilt.

"We're here," Mitch said.

Cornelia was embarrassed that she had not noticed.

"You don't have to do this," Mitch said. In the mirror, he watched her press her lips together, making her square chin look even more stern. The tight bun in her iron-gray hair did nothing to soften her features. "I could take those letters in for you and leave them with Sheriff Bowden."

Her answer was an abrupt "No."

Cornelia opened the car door and stepped out into the morning sunlight. One deep breath to clear the cobwebs from her mind, and then she marched into Sheriff Bowden's office.

Bowden looked up. "Miss Pettijohn, I wasn't expecting to see you again. Is something wrong?"

"Nothing new. I came to see Rosemary."

His eyebrows rose. "You think that's wise? I mean—under the circumstances?"

"I doubt that it's wise, but it is important. May I see her?"

Bowden opened his mouth to speak. The resolute expression in Cornelia's eyes stopped his tongue. One steel wheel of his office chair squeaked as he pushed himself back from the desk and stood up. "I'll ask. Don't be surprised if she refuses to see you. After last night, she won't want anything to do with either of us."

Cornelia didn't respond. She was all too aware of the role she played in Rosemary Carson's confession. There was no reason for her to feel guilty about uncovering the truth. The Carsons were perfectly willing to let her uncle rot in jail for a crime he didn't commit. Still, she had seen the ravages of savin poisoning on a young woman. If that poison was given to someone she loved—well, she didn't know what she would have done. She hoped not murder.

Sheriff Bowden closed the door between the jail and his office.

The sound jarred her from her thoughts. "Well?"

"She said she'd see you." He glanced at the large black leather purse Cornelia carried. "If you have your pistol in there, you'd best leave your pocketbook on my desk."

"I left it with Mitch," Cornelia said. She smiled for the first time that he could remember. "I'm not planning to assist with a jail break, I promise."

Cornelia Pettijohn had the kind of smile that lit her face from the inside. It didn't make her features attractive by any stretch of the imagination, but the warmth surprised Bowden. If they had met under other circumstances, if he had seen her smile instead of glower at him through every conversation, they might have become friends.

He cleared his throat. "I didn't think you would."

Cornelia pointed at the door. "May I?"

Bowden held the door for her. She stepped past him and glanced down the row of cells to the one housing Rosemary Carson. Her husband, William, was standing outside her cell. His suitcoat hung from the back of a wooden chair. One arm was pushed through the bars and wrapped around his wife's shoulders. Cornelia could see Rosemary's fingers clinging to his ribs. Neither of them moved.

Part of her resisted entering the windowless room, repressive with the scents of stale sweat and chlorine bleach. She willed her feet forward. Her words were forced, awkward on her tongue. "Hello, Rosemary, Mr. Carson."

Carson hugged his wife closer and gave her a slight nod of recognition.

Cornelia didn't know what she had expected. The defeat in their faces hurt more than the anger. "I brought these for you," she said, as she reached into her bag and pulled out two small bundles of letters.

William Carson recoiled as if she were holding a live rattlesnake in her outstretched hand.

"Rosemary, please—" Her voice broke. "I know there isn't going to be a trial. Maybe that's for the best. It would be awful for the children."

Rosemary gasped.

"Haven't you done enough harm?" her husband snapped. "Leave us alone."

Cornelia took a step closer to them. Her voice took on its usual gruff tone. "This stack of letters are to the court, asking for leniency in sentencing, and stating what we know of Mr. Janzen's actions. Uncle Percival, Mr. Rowley, even Sheriff Bowden's son want to do what they can to mitigate your wife's sentencing. These," she added, as she indicated the larger batch of letters, "are to the governor asking clemency. There will be more; Mr. Janzen's father is asking the members of his congregation to write on her behalf. Mrs. Minyard left town before we thought of a way to help, but Uncle Percival has sent her a telegram. I am sure she will do what she can. Mr. Rowley is on the telephone contacting members of his unit this morning, asking them to join the effort."

Rosemary's mouth gaped open.

Cornelia slapped the letters down in the empty chair and turned to go.

"Wait! Please Cornelia, don't go."

Tears dripped down Rosemary Carson's face. She brushed them away with one hand. "William, would you and the sheriff give us a few minutes alone?"

"Are you sure?"

She nodded. "We'll be fine. Please." Rosemary slipped out of his embrace and watched as he walked away. When the door closed behind him she moved closer to Cornelia.

"Cornelia, I am so sorry about the trouble the savin caused your uncle. William found it in my bag the night Mr. Janzen died. He was horrified when he realized what I had done. We had an awful fight. He took the bottle and stormed out. I don't know what he did with it, but when it turned up in your uncle's room, he said that your uncle would be cleared eventually, and that I should be thinking of my children. I didn't leave when I should have because I wasn't as confident that they would free him."

She lifted her chin and looked into Cornelia's eyes. "If you tell a soul, I'll deny everything. I confessed to planting the bottle myself to keep my children from losing both parents."

Chapter 17

Professor Pettijohn spotted Rowley talking to one of the departing couples outside the lodge. He waited for the young man to finish his business before waving him over.

"Good afternoon, Professor. I hear you are leaving us soon. I suppose the events of the last few days have cooled your interest in property."

"I enjoyed meeting the jailer. The accommodations left much to be desired, though. I'm getting a little old to be comfortable on a jailhouse mattress." The old gent's blue eyes crinkled at the corners when he chuckled. "As for the local real estate, there is one piece of property I was hoping you would show me before my niece returns."

Rowley's face brightened. "Which parcel is that, sir?"

"The one you want for your lodge."

"That isn't part of the new development," the young man said swiftly. "The guy who owns the property doesn't even like seeing all this construction."

The professor put a hand on his shoulder. "Mr. Rowley, I have no desire to buy the property out from under you. I would like to see the place you want and hear about your plans for the future."

Surprise, then a smile from the land agent. "In that case, I would love to show you around. It isn't far from here, but there's no road that direction. We'll have to travel by boat. Are you up to that, Professor?"

"I've made several boat trips during my stay in Homosassa."

Rowley's smile broadened. "I'll bet none of those trips was aboard a 22-foot runabout."

The old man's white eyebrows lifted. "Are you a racer?"

"No, mine is designed for fishing, even has a small cabin, but she's the fastest thing on the river."

"Sounds like an excellent way to travel. I would love to get some film of it. Could I impose upon you to bring my camera along?"

"That's no imposition at all, Professor. The Fisherman's Dream will be beautiful in your film."

Professor Pettijohn beamed.

"Are the ladies joining us?" Rowley asked, as they walked toward the professor's room.

Professor Pettijohn paused to think about that question. "Cornelia left for Ocala early this morning. The water pump for our vehicle was finally replaced. She left us to pack while she was away." He chuckled. "You can see how hard we are working on that chore. I'm sure Teddy will enjoy the prospect of an outing on the river."

Cornelia Pettijohn was an awful passenger. Her friend, Miss Lawless, was fun-loving and talkative. Not Miss Cornelia; it was hard to get more than three words from her at a time. She sat in stoic silence, her posture rigid, her eyes on the road ahead. Mitch wasn't sure why he had offered to drive her all the way to Ocala. This morning's drive to Inverness was dull enough.

Maybe it was guilt. Sticking close to her had given him a wealth of material for his newspaper. Thanks to the Pettijohns, he no longer needed to keep up the charade of being down on his luck and desperate enough to come all the way to Homosassa to find work. The West Coast Development Company was losing him as a driver as soon as he got back from this junket. He needed to get this story finished before someone else scooped him. In the time this drive took, he could have hammered out a good-sized column on events of the past few days. Shoot, thanks to the Pettijohns he had enough material to write a whole series of articles.

He wasn't sure how much to tell his readers about the professor's remarkable memory. They might not believe him. He wouldn't have believed it if he hadn't witnessed the old gent in action. Even without that detail, he had plenty to work with: two murders, the rackets trying to muscle in on the new casino, shootouts, arrests—just the thought of putting those things down on paper made him drive faster.

"Easy, Mitch," he told himself as he shifted down to make the turn onto the Dixie Highway. Hours on the road might pass in a more congenial way with the professor or Miss Lawless along for the ride, but his newspaper wouldn't reimburse a speeding ticket.

Too bad Cornelia didn't inherit her uncle's sense of humor. Was "inherit" the right word? A niece wasn't a direct descendant, but humor had to be somewhere in the family tree.

"Look out," Cornelia shouted.

Ahead of them, half a dozen colored men in the familiar grey and white striped prison uniforms worked a few feet apart. Mitch swung wide to avoid hitting the shackled men. "Sorry, ma'am. I should have expected that. Florida chain gangs are always working on the roads somewhere."

"I've noticed."

Her flat tone gave him no clue of her opinion. They lapsed into silence again. This was going to be a longest thirty-mile drive in history.

They had just crossed the Marion County line when Cornelia spotted another group of prisoners cutting thick vines and underbrush away from the road. The legs of their striped trousers were caked in mud almost to the knees. No doubt they were standing in several inches of water. It looked like miserable work.

"Are those corrugated steel sheds some sort of movable privy?" she asked.

Mitch hesitated a few seconds before answering. "They're sweatboxes."

"What?"

"When a prisoner gets out of line or lazy, they put him in the sweatbox as punishment." He didn't look at Cornelia. The disapproval in that one word made him want to hang his head in shame. "It's not so bad in winter."

Cornelia looked back at the tiny metal box. It couldn't be more than four feet square and so squat that a tall man would have to stoop to keep from banging his head on the roof. "Not so bad. Indeed. When does it get bad to be stuffed in an airless box in the Florida sun, when the heat turns metal walls into a roasting pan, or when a body is dehydrated to the point of delirium?"

She knew her voice was rising. She didn't care. Her uncle had fought a war to end slavery. Prisoners had no rights. Slavery was the only word she could think of that fit this barbaric situation.

"Look, ma'am, I don't like it any more than you do. It isn't right that men like those built about every road in the state. Some of them are hardened criminals, most are locked up because the county needs land cleared or roads widened."

"You're a newsman. Speak up. Do something."

Mitch fought back the urge to use profanity. He pushed moist locks of black hair back from his forehead. Wind from the open car window blew them back onto his brow. "I don't own the paper. I just work there," he said. "Now and then I manage to slip in a line or two that my editor doesn't strike. Believe me, that's rare. The paper isn't going to print stories that rankle advertisers."

Cornelia fumed, because she knew he was right. When it came to a choice between free speech and paid advertisements, money won. She was angry at her own lack of power to make a difference. She wondered if her upcoming retirement was a mistake. In the wards, she had the authority to change the way her nurses did their jobs. Sometimes she could even influence the doctors, although she did her best to make them think the change was their idea. The rest of the world was a chaotic mess. Maybe she wasn't cut out for civilian life.

"Miss Pettijohn, I do try."

His statement jolted her from her thoughts. It took a second to grasp that he was talking about the chain gang. A trace of a smile played at the corners of her mouth. "I believe you."

190

The reporter almost laughed. "From you, ma'am, those three words are lavish praise."

"Is that your boat?" Teddy asked, as they approached the Homosassa dock. The sleek polished mahogany boat she'd pointed out was unlike any boat she had ever seen.

"That's her," Rowley said, his voice filled with pride. He shifted the camera tripod off his shoulder and set it up for the professor. "A genuine 1914 runabout. You wouldn't know it now, but the Fisherman's Dream was pretty battered when I bought her. I've spent most of the past year restoring her to her pre-war glory."

"She's certainly beautiful," Teddy said.

Professor Pettijohn was more interested in mechanics than shine. "What kind of motor does she have?"

"The old engine was beyond repair. I replaced it with one of the new Chrysler Imperial six cylinders. Runs like a dream."

Teddy climbed aboard the boat and arranged her hat to a more fetching angle for the professor's film. Cornelia was going to be mad enough to spit when she found out what the two of them had done while she was away. It served her right for leaving them at the lodge while she went gallivanting with Mitch.

Rowley cast off the line holding him to the pier, and joined her on the boat. "You might want to hold on to your hat, Miss Lawless. The professor wants me to take the boat for a turn or two for his moving picture." He started the engine. "It may get windy back there."

He backed out of the slip and took a slow turn to head upriver. Just past the fish house, he turned around and started picking up speed.

They cruised past the professor waving, and laughing for the camera.

Rowley slowed down as they neared the bend of the river, made another graceful turn, and brought his sleek motorboat back to where the professor stood filming them. Once he was back in the boat slip, he left the engine idling and climbed out to help the professor with the camera. Soon, the three of them were gliding over the clear spring-fed river past sawgrass marshland and thick cypress groves.

"There it is, Professor," Rowley shouted above the roar of the engine. "What do you think?"

Teddy looked in the direction he was pointing. A small fishing pier jutted out from the riverbank. Beyond it, the land rose a few feet. An overgrown path led through half a dozen live oaks to a dilapidated house that made Mr. Scroggins' rustic cabin look well maintained. She was grateful that he hadn't asked her opinion. The place looked like a good breeze could blow the roof off.

"The important question, Peter, is what do you think?" the professor replied. "When you look up that bank, what do you see?"

Peter Rowley shoved his sandy hair back from his brow. "Two hundred and twenty-five acres of prime hunting land with about every type of game a man could want, a spring-fed river pumping thousands of gallons of fresh clear water into the Gulf of Mexico every day. Within minutes, the Fisherman's Dream could take half a dozen guests to the Gulf for saltwater fishing. Upstream, there's fresh water fishing. From here down, the water gets more and more brackish. Every sort of fishing is minutes away. Up there, where the old house is, there should be a lodge with porches so folks can watch the sunset and sunrise. Not one of those fancy lodges for rich folks; one built of real Florida cedar, logs and bare beams."

He stopped talking, and color crept up his neck. "I didn't mean to go on about the place. I guess you think I'm being foolish."

Professor Pettijohn reached into his breast pocket and pulled out a thick envelope. "I brought this to purchase a winter property. I think it would be much better spent investing in your dream."

Rowley's face paled. "I can't take your money. It wouldn't be right."

"Consider it an investment. We can draw up papers if you want, a loan or a silent partnership. I have spent most of my life educating and encouraging young men to pursue their dreams, to look at what is possible and make it real. You have

192

a good dream. I would be honored to play a part in your plans for this land." He pressed the envelope into Peter Rowley's hand.

"I'm hungry," Mitch said as he pulled into the parking lot of a small restaurant on the outskirts of Ocala. "Can I treat you to dinner before we part ways?"

The hand-painted sign above the entrance proclaimed that they served "The Best Frankfurters and Freshest Seafood in Florida". Cornelia hesitated as she mulled over her response. The odd combination of specialties didn't bother her. She'd seen worse.

Her mind didn't know what to make of Mitch's invitation. Attractive young men did not, as the French said, *invite une femme d'un certain âge* to dinner unless she were a near relative. Besides, she would have sworn that Mitch was eager to be rid of her. In the end, curiosity won over her suspicions. She nodded consent.

Halfway through his second plate of fish and chips, Mitch looked up and gave her a sheepish grin. "I did say I was hungry."

"Indeed."

"Can I get you anything else? Maybe a slice of their key lime pie?"

Cornelia shook her head.

"Mind if I have a slice?"

"Go ahead," she said. The truth was she had enjoyed the enthusiasm he'd shown attacking his food. His grin, his tousled black hair, and the constant shadow of a beard reminded Cornelia of her father, except for the dark brown eyes. Cornelius Pettijohn's eyes had been the same brilliant shade of blue as his brother Percival's—and her own.

"Can I ask you a question?"

Her eyes narrowed. "You just did," Cornelia replied.

"True enough. But what I wanted to ask is: after fighting like the devil to clear your uncle, you turned around and tried to help Mrs. Carson. Why? I'd be livid if someone framed my uncle."

Cornelia's brow furrowed. "Mrs. Carson was livid. Look where that led."

"You can't tell me you don't get angry," he said. "You were mad as a bee in a bottle over those men today."

"I have a frightful temper."

"Not with Mrs. Carson. Once you got her to confess, you set about trying to get her out of the mess she's in."

"You think she should rot in jail."

Mitch frowned. "She committed cold-blooded murder."

The waitress arrived with Mitch's pie and the check.

Cornelia waited until she was out of earshot. "I would think it was rather hot blooded," she said. "The rage she held over Janzen's role in her sister's death was a banked fire. When she discovered Janzen was going to be at that land sale, the flame consumed her. She blocked out everything else. Her husband, her children, her life vanished from her thoughts. Her world narrowed to Janzen and her sister."

"You feel sorry for her."

"No. I understand her desire to give Janzen a dose of the drug he gave her sister. She saw it as poetic justice. If she had taken a moment to think what that kind of justice would do to the other people she loved... I feel sorry for her children. They love her. They need her. Those children are the real casualties of her private war."

Mitch was puzzled. "You care that much about children you've never met?"

"Yes. I care that they will lose the rest of their childhood. Those children will be teased and tormented by their peers, and made to pay a thousand times over for their mother's crime. Rosemary needs clemency for their sake."

"Who would have thought that Miss Cornelia Pettijohn had a soft spot for children?"

"Even I was a child once; not one who got on well with other children, though," Cornelia replied.

Mitch didn't know what to say. In school, he was as guilty as anyone else in teasing odd or plain classmates. It had seemed harmless then. The look in Miss Cornelia's eyes told him that old hurts still lingered.

194

He scraped the last of his pie from the plate and lifted it to his mouth. "That was outstanding. Are you sure you won't have a slice before we go?"

"You enjoyed it enough for the both of us."

Cornelia was impressed. The mechanic had cleaned as well as repaired her sedan. Every inch of metal gleamed in the late afternoon sunlight. The leather was buffed to a fine sheen. Even the tires looked clean. Her automobile hadn't looked this good since she drove it from the Dodge Brothers showroom.

"Is that your uncle's vehicle?" Mitch asked.

Cornelia bristled. "No. It's mine."

"Sorry. I didn't mean to offend. The way Professor Pettijohn talks—I thought it was his."

"I've noticed," Cornelia said.

Mitch chuckled. "I'm going to miss the old guy. He's quite a character."

"Isn't your paper in St. Petersburg? Perhaps you could join us for dinner one evening. We'll be staying at the Vinoy Park Hotel for the next week."

Mitch whistled. "That's a little out of my class, Miss Pettijohn. A meal there would cost me a week's pay."

"Really?"

"The hotel's only been opened since New Year's Eve, but the guest list supplies half our society columns."

Cornelia wondered if her uncle knew. Perhaps he had booked the fancy hotel for his birthday. Too bad matters in Homosassa had quashed that. He'd worked hard enough earning his money. It was good that he was getting to enjoy some of the rewards of his labor.

"If you change your mind, you know where to find us," Cornelia said as she climbed out of the Cadillac.

She started to close the door, paused and leaned in, "Thank you, for everything. I don't know what would have happened without your help."

Mitch pressed his lips together and nodded.

She closed the door and walked into the garage.

Cornelia slipped behind the wheel of her sedan, stepped on the clutch, and turned the key. The engine rumbled to life. She shifted into gear and pulled away from the curb. She turned the corner onto the Dixie Highway and let the car pick up speed. She shifted again and stepped on the gas. For the next couple of hours, she was going to sit back and enjoy the peace and quiet of being absolutely alone.

THE END

The Mary Pickford Cocktail

One unexpected consequence of Prohibition was the large
number of American bartenders who found work in Cuba.
Eddie Woelke and Fred Kaufmann were both among the
bartending refugees tending bar at the Hotel National de
Cuba. Woelke, the senior bartender, claimed credit for
inventing the Mary Pickford cocktail, but Kaufmann was
better known for using fresh pineapple juice in his drinks. In
1928 Basil Woon, not known for his accuracy, gave the credit
to Kaufman in his book *When It's Cocktail Time in Cuba*. We
may never know for certain which of them invented the Mary
Pickford in honor of the film star's 1922 visit to Cuba, where
she spent the winter with her husband, actor Douglas
Fairbanks.

Another point of contention over the cocktail arose from not
writing the recipe down. The first know written recipe for the
drink appeared nearly seven years later and did not contain
the signature Italian Maraschino liqueur. The version served
at the Hotel National de Cuba is made with white rum and
Maraschino liqueur, as does the version in the International
Bartender's Association official guide. Drinkers will have to
decide for themselves which way the cocktail should be made.

Mary Pickford Cocktail
(*1 shot = 1 ounce = 60 ml)

2 shots white rum
1 1/2 shots fresh pineapple juice
1/4 shot grenadine
 1/8 shot Maraschino liqueur

Pour over chipped ice, shake, and strain into a large chilled cocktail glass. Garnish with a wedge of fresh pineapple, a maraschino cherry, or both. Serve straight up.

Information on the Mary Pickford Cocktail recipe comes from the HavanaClub.com and the Hotel National de Cuba website.

Authors' Notes

Homosassa

Native Americans were the first inhabitants of the area that became **Homosassa**. The Armed Occupation Act of 1842, which granted 160 acres of land to any head of a family or single man who could bear arms, led to the settlement of Homosassa by homesteaders. William Cooley was the first prominent citizen of the new town. He sold his property to David Levy Yulee in 1851. Yulee had his slaves clear a thousand acres for a plantation and sugar mill along the Homosassa River. Yulee was the first Jew to serve in Congress, but his career and the plantation both ended with the Civil War.

Homosassa inspired dreams long before the West Coast Development Company. Northern investors purchased Yulee's land in 1884 and, as the newly-formed Homosassa Company, platted their new property for a city set up in the neoclassical tradition. It was never fully developed, but the town attracted many important tourists: Grover Cleveland, John Jacob Astor, and other notables.

The West Coast Development Company

The **West Coast Development Company** was formed in 1924 by H.S. and Bruce L. Hoover, along with over 700 associates. The Company quietly purchased a reported 142 miles of Gulf frontage and its associates held $200,000,000 in combined wealth at the time New Homosassa was introduced.

Homosassa Springs

New Homosassa, better known as **Homosassa Springs**, was built slightly west of the original fishing village of Homosassa. The city designer was Harland Bartholomew, best known for being the first city planner for St. Louis, Missouri. Promotions painted the picture of a shining utopia rising from an emerald jungle. "Homosassa, Miracle City," one advertisement read, with a list of "Moral and Financial Endorsements." "Plans are laid for an ultimate city of 100,000 people," a brochure from the Chamber of Commerce announced. The fertility of the hammock land, the "almost exhaustless source of lumber and lumber products", and the spectacular abundance of fish, waterfowl, and wild game were among the selling points. The advantages of the location were as advertised, but Homosassa Springs never reached the projected population size of the brochure.

The Mullet Express

In December 1888, the Silver Springs, Ocala and Gulf Railroad opened a spur line from Ocala to Homosassa. They named the line the "Dunnellon Short," but to locals it is forever the **Mullet Express**. For more than forty years the "Mullet Express" pulled out of Homosassa Station at 6:30 AM each weekday loaded with mullet, logs, Spanish moss, mail, passengers and bootlegged whiskey headed to northern markets.

Homosassa station's small sidetrack was abuzz with workers long before dawn. In the days before ice was readily available, the fish was dried and packed in barrels that had to be hand loaded into railcars. Later, the barrels were replaced by large bins that were filled nightly with fresh fish packed in layers of ice and loaded onto the train before it left town. Both methods involved backbreaking work that had to be finished on schedule.

Each evening Engine 501 returned carrying the mail, merchandise for local businesses, and tourists keen of visiting the famed "sportsman's paradise" in and around Florida's Homosassa River. Occasionally, a private Pullman owned by some of the wealthier sportsmen was added to the rear of the train in Ocala to be sidetracked in Homosassa for the duration of their visit. Sportsmen's guides as far back as 1890 mention trips to Homosassa aboard these private luxury cars.

The steam locomotive, its two passenger cars, flatcar, and mail car made a final last run in November of 1941. Old Engine 501 was scrapped along with the railcars and tracks to provide much needed metal for WWII war effort. Today Homosassa Springs State Park is host to a modernized version of the locomotive, the new 'Mullet Express" was designed from photographs and harkens back to the old train's history, delivering a recorded message about the Express to park visitors.

The Atlanta Fishing Club and the Chauffeur's Cabin

A group of some two dozen prominent businessmen and sportsmen from Atlanta, Georgia formed **The Atlanta Fishing Club** in 1899. One of the club activities was an annual fishing trip to the banks of the Homosassa River. The group purchased land, and in 1903 built a clubhouse for the use of current and future members. The two-story wood frame house features Victorian Revival decorative gable ends. It has been altered and added to several times, but it remains a private club owned and visited by the same Georgia families that founded the club.

One of the early and most difficult additions to make was a **chauffeur's cabin** near the main house. Homosassa had a clearly posted sign on the highway at the outskirts of town informing the public that, for their own safety, colored people were not permitted within the city limits after sundown. An exception was made for the chauffeurs on the condition that they not leave the cabin after dark. Until the Jim Crow laws were overturned, this tiny cabin was the only place in Homosassa where a black man could spend the night. Unlike the clubhouse, the chauffeur's cabin no longer stands on the original site. When club members wished to have the cabin removed, it was adopted by local history buff Jim Anderson and moved to the backyard of his Olde Mill House printing museum. He uses the front porch of the cabin as the stage for an annual music festival and has even written a blues number about one of the chauffeurs who autographed the walls of the old cabin.

Binder Boys

Binder boys ('binder' sometimes pronounced to rhyme with 'tinder') were generally young men who started transactions for a piece of land and took the binder, also known as the down payment, from the buyer of a piece of property. Some binder boys were used by land agents who needed assistance in handling the glut of transactions during the Florida Land Boom, but others were entrepreneurs who placed the first binder on a property themselves, then resold it at a higher value to the next customer.

Kit Houses

Kit houses were also known as mail order homes, pre-cut homes, or catalog homes. As 'mail order' suggests, these were houses that could be ordered for delivery. The kit contained all the lumber and materials necessary to construct the house, with the frequent exception of mortar, bricks, or other items needed to build the foundation. The buyer usually hired local workers to handle this last part.

During the early twentieth century, Sears and Roebuck sold a large number of kit houses, as did Sterling Homes and Harris Homes. The materials were shipped by rail to the desired location and assembled by workers. Anything from a simple cottage or a two-story house with porches could be ordered from catalogs.

Most homes were of the standard 'box' variety, but in late 1925 The Aladdin Company bought some property in south Florida, where they intended to construct **Aladdin City**, a town with Moorish-style buildings. In January of 1926, they had a 'dawn to dusk' demonstration where they built an entire house on opening day. Construction petered out quickly with the end of the Florida Land Boom, but some of the structures lasted until the 1980s, when Hurricane Andrew dealt serious damage to the area.

Medicinal Alcohol

Prohibition didn't ban the use of alcoholic beverages in all circumstances. A medical loophole was also created in the Volstead Act for the therapeutic prescribing of alcohol. As a result, **medicinal alcohol**, also known as *Spiritus frumenti*, was prescribed throughout Prohibition.

Under the provisions of this loophole, only a physician with a permit could write a prescription for medicinal alcohol. The dose of this medical dispensation was limited to one pint every ten days. The government issued books of specially designed forms for this purpose, and the designs were changed often to outstrip counterfeiters.

Economist Clark Warburton stated that the consumption of medicinal alcohol increased by 400 percent during the 1920s. By 1929, there were 116,756 physicians in the twenty-six states that permitted the use of medicinal alcohol. According to the Journal of the American Medical Association, about half of those physicians were prescribing it for patients.

Real People

Ignacio Antinori (February 17, 1885 – October 23, 1940),
Tampa's earliest Italian mafia boss, was born in Palermo,
Sicily. He emigrated to the United States with his family in the
early 1900s. By the 1930s, Antinori had established a narcotics
pipeline, one of the largest in the country, from the Cuban
gangs in Tampa to the Kansas City Mafia. His family was later
subsumed by the Trafficante family.

During the mid-1920s, Antinori challenged Charlie Wall for
control of organized crime in the Tampa Bay region, kicking
off the "Era of Blood". The rivalry lasted for about a decade.
In early 1940, Antinori brought Kansas City hitmen in to kill
Charlie Wall. It was the third attempt on Wall's life, though,
and he was cagey enough to survive. Antinori's murder later
that year, however, was not Wall's revenge. The story that
surfaced was that Antinori sent a shipment of bad narcotics to
the Chicago Mafia. They were displeased, to say the least, and
demanded a refund. Antinori refused, and his funeral was
closed-casket.

Basil Orville Bowden (November 15, 1868 – April 30, 1938)
was the sheriff of Citrus County during the time this book is
set. Bowden lost his father when he was only three months old
and his mother at the tender age of six. He rose above the
adversity of his early life through honesty and hard work, first
as a farmer, then a newspaper publisher. In 1904 he
established the *Dade City Star* and ran the paper until he sold

it in 1915. He moved to Inverness and became owner and editor of the *Citrus County Chronicle*.

His reputation as a man of exceptional integrity and a solid business background led to his being appointed county sheriff in 1917 in the hopes he could salvage the office from financial ruin. In a year's time he reversed the deficit, reduced the debt, and put the affairs of the office in order. Throughout his career he ran the sheriff's office efficiently and economically. He was considered by his peers to be the best sheriff in the state of Florida.

In addition to his duties as sheriff, he also served as chair of the county draft board. Bowden took pride in the fact that his own sons volunteered for service in WWI instead of waiting to be called. He viewed service a responsibility of citizenship. The character of "Sheriff Bowden" in this book is entirely a work of fiction. While we have endeavored to keep the character true to the reputation of the actual person, the events and conversations, the personality and mannerisms are all made up for the sake of telling a good story. There is no relationship between the fictional sheriff and the true Sheriff Bowden beyond using his name.

Charles Arthur "Dazzy" Vance (March 4, 1891 – February 16, 1961) was a professional baseball player who pitched for five Major League franchises, including the Brooklyn Dodgers. He was best known for his fastball and the "three men on third" incident in 1926 where he and two other players tried to occupy third base at the same time. Vance first visited Florida for spring training, but found many other reasons to return. He had a great love for fishing and hunting, and Citrus County became his permanent home. Vance purchased the Homosassa Hotel from the West Coast Development Company in 1930 and entertained many of his friends there. Vance was inducted into the Baseball Hall of Fame in 1955.

Charles McKay "Charlie" Wall (March 10, 1880 – April 18, 1955) also known as "The Dean of the Underworld," "The White Shadow," and "The Unofficial Mayor of Tampa".

It is impossible to write about prohibition around Tampa Bay without mentioning Charlie Wall. Charlie's father was a Tampa civic leader and prominent physician, but obligations left little time for family life. Charlie lost his beloved mother at a young age. His father soon remarried, but less than a year into the marriage he died, leaving Charlie in the hands of a stepmother he detested. At the age of twelve Charlie shot her with a .22 caliber rifle, an act that landed him in military school.

At the age of thirteen, he was kicked out of school for visiting a brothel. Going home to his stepmother was out of the question. Instead, Charlie made own his way in the rough and tumble shanty town of Fort Brooke, a former military base infamous for gambling, drugs, and bawdy houses. Charlie was smart, ambitious, unafraid, naturally gifted in mathematics, and had a head for business. The scrappy kid earned the attention of the grownups in Tampa's illegal establishments, and from them he learned the ins and outs of the rackets. He also brought to the table his knowledge of Tampa politics and elite society. He looked and dressed the part of an up and coming businessman.

Charlie used his newfound gambling skills to amass wealth and rise to the top of Tampa's criminal underworld. He used his name and political connections to stay there. His power was so far-reaching, that he was often referred to as the unofficial mayor of Tampa. Nobody got elected in the Bay Area without his approval. By the 1920's, Charlie Wall was at the pinnacle of success. "The Dean of the Underworld" used his unique combination of organizational skills and political connections to virtually monopolize the bolita racket. Gambling in general was under Charlie's thumb, as were prostitution and bootlegging. His El Dorado Casino was a gilded example of his power, combining all three rackets under one roof. Charlie was boss of every racket around Tampa Bay and throughout central Florida, except for drugs. Early in his climb to power, he made a deal with the Cubans to leave that racket to them.

Sources for More Information:

The Way It Was: Race Relations and Integration in Citrus County, Florida by Dennis Shawn Allen. Florida State University Digital Library, 2013.
History of Florida: Past and Present, Historical and Biographical, Volume 2 by Harry Gardner Cutler. Lewis Publishing Company, 1923.
Cigar City Mafia - A Complete History of the Tampa Underworld, written by Scott M. Deitche. Barricade Books, 2004. ASIN 8004449516.
Images of America: Citrus County by Lynn M. Homan, Thomas Reilly. Arcadia Publishing, 2001. ISBN 0-7385-0679-6.
Private History in Public: Exhibition and the Settings of Everyday Life by Tammy Stone-Gordon. Rowman & Littlefield, 2010. ISBN 9780759119352.

Hallock, Charles. The Fishing Tourist. Forest and Stream Quarterly, Fall 1891
"Homosassa is Greatest Development on West Coast" by Bennett Roach, St. Petersburg Times, 2/18/1926
Homosassa: "Museum Proprietor Prizes Cabin," Citrus County Chronicle, 6/26/2011

Sarasota Herald-Tribune advertisement, 01/17/1926.

"Homosassa: A City in the Building." Chamber of Commerce, Homosassa, Florida, 1926. University of Florida Digital Collections.
Homosassa Civic Club. Florida Humanities Council Brochure - Historic Homosassa

http://www.homosassahistory.com/
http://cigarcitymagazine.com/charlie-wall-tampas-organized-crime-kingpin/
http://mafia.wikia.com/wiki/Charlie_Wall
http://americanmafia.com/Feature_Articles_19.html
http://epmonthly.com/blog/whiskey-prescriptions-and-the-prohibition-act/
http://www.greenhousebistromarket.com/history/

About the Authors

Hair and Photo by Jay Martello

Gwen Mayo is passionate about blending her loves of history and mystery fiction. She currently lives and writes in Safety Harbor, Florida, but grew up in a large Irish family in the hills of Eastern Kentucky. She is the author of the Nessa Donnelly Mysteries and co-author of the Three Snowbirds stories with Sarah Glenn.

Her stories have appeared in A Whodunit Halloween, Decades of Dirt, Halloween Frights (Volume I), and several flash fiction collections. She belongs to Sisters in Crime, SinC Guppies, the Short Mystery Fiction Society, the Historical Novel Society, the Independent Book Publishers Association and the Florida Authors and Publishers Association.

Gwen has a bachelor's degree in political science from the University of Kentucky. Her most interesting job, though, was as a brakeman and railroad engineer from 1983 - 1987. She was one of the last engineers to be certified on steam locomotives.

Sarah E. Glenn has a B.S. in Journalism, which is a great degree for the dilettante she is. Later on, she did a stint as a graduate student in classical languages. She didn't get the degree, but she's great with crosswords. Her most interesting job was working the reports desk for the police department in Lexington, Kentucky, where she learned that criminals really are dumb.

Her great-great aunt served as a nurse in WWI, and was injured by poison gas during the fighting. A hundred years later, this would inspire Sarah to write stories Aunt Dess would probably not approve of.

Her short stories appear in State of Horror: Louisiana, Hoosier Hoops and Hijinks, Fish Tales: The Guppy Anthology, and many other story collections. She belongs to Sisters in Crime, SinC Guppies, the Short Mystery Fiction Society, and the Historical Novel Society. She lives in Safety Harbor, Florida.